Pure Poetry

BINNIE
KIRSHENBAUM

Simon & Schuster

Simon & Schuster
Rockefeller Center
1230 Avenue of the Americas
New York, NY 10020

Designed by Kyoko Watanabe

Manufactured in the United States of America

10 9 8 7 6 5 4 3 2 1

Library of Congress Cataloging-In-Publication Data
Kirshenbaum, Binnie.
Pure Poetry / Binnie Kirshenbaum.
p.   cm.
1. Jews—United States—Fiction.   I. Title.
PS3561.I775 P87 2000
813'.54 21—dc21   99-045323

ISBN 0-7432-4182-7

For information regarding the special discounts for bulk purchases, please contact Simon &
Schuster Special Sales at 1-800-456-6798 or business@simonandschuster.com

Acknowledgments

The title of the novel and all of the chapter titles were selected from the *Princeton Encyclopedia of Poetry and Poetics,* edited by Alex Preminger, with four exceptions. The chapters "Free Verse," "Katauta," and "Cynghanedd Draws" were defined in *The New Book of Forms* by Lewis Turco, and the definition for "Pastoral" came from "A Glossary of Literary Terms," revised by M. H. Abrams.

The author also thanks her friends, her loved ones—Tony Gidari, Susan Montez, Maureen Howard, Laurie Stone, Nic and Connie Christopher, Ross Harrison, Thomas Thornton, Susan Wheeler, Lutz Wolff—for their insights and inspirations, and many thanks to Roz Siegel.

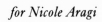

for Nicole Aragi

Pure Poetry is a prescriptive rather than a descriptive term in that it designates not an actual body of verse but a theoretical ideal to which poetry may aspire.

Pure Poetry

1

scansion: The system of describing conventional poetic rhythms by visual symbols for metrical analysis and study. Stressed and unstressed syllables are marked according to the degree of sense emphasis transmitted. It does not make rhythm; it reveals it by transferring it from a temporal into a spatial dimension.

WITH THE SPLENDOR DERIVED from pointillistic detail, I'm getting a picture regarding Henry's ex-wife. Our first date, and already I am privy to the particulars of the marital dirt. Is this a treat for me or what? Ah, those trifling morsels of delectability. Minutiae like candy-kisses. Henry tells me how Dawn lets the children go without bathing for days at a clip. How graciously and with a tra-la-la of *oh-it-was-nothing*, she accepts compliments on dinners she did not prepare, but rather bought from the caterer at Dean & Deluca. How her nipples are cylinder shaped and long like Olive Oyl's nose, and how her pubic hair grows to extraordinary lengths.

"I swear to you," Henry says, "it grew like you wouldn't believe. Honest, it was like the hair on your head except that it was scraggly. You have beautiful hair. The way the light catches it." Henry takes a sip of his drink, a gin and tonic, and he asks, "What color is it exactly? Your hair? On your passport what does it say about hair color?"

"Black Cherry." I tell him my hair color is Black Cherry. That is what it says on the bottle, but I don't tell him that part. That it is Black Cherry by L'Oréal. Instead, I steer the conversation back to where it was before he digressed. The color of my hair is of no compelling interest to me at the moment. I much prefer the dish on his ex-wife. "So what does Dawn look like?" I ask. "Is she very beautiful? Aside from the nipple issue, that is."

Henry shifts forward in his seat to get at his wallet. Our table is window-side, and a glimmer of my reflection stares back at me, sizing me up. I spook myself and turn away from the window, as if you could turn your back on your double. Henry hands me the photograph of his ex-wife. She is all dolled up. "For a wedding," he tells me. "Mostly she dresses like a slob. Sweatpants and grimy T-shirts. And she doesn't put on fresh underwear daily either. To tell you the truth"—Henry's voice drops a notch as if he is confessing to a crime—"her personal hygiene is not the best. I'll bet you're clean," he says. "You look like you are very clean."

I bring the photograph near to my nose. I'm myopic like nobody's business, an affliction that can also translate into a lack of discernment. Vanity prohibits me from wearing my glasses except when the need to see clearly is a crucial one. Twenty-twenty vision is not sufficient motivation to obscure my eyes, which are the size of walnuts and hazel colored. Not to mention I was blessed with lashes like Liza Minnelli, only mine are real, and don't even talk to me about contact lenses because the eye is not an orifice.

I focus on the subject of the photograph. Seated on a lawn chair, her legs crossed, she is wearing a yellow frock and a straw hat with a wide brim. Her smile is also wide, and if I squint, I can make out that her teeth are crooked. She is a skinny woman, and she is not much to look at. Although she might be pretty enough if not for the lack of a chin, which is the most serious of all the facial flaws.

We did not meet that way, but Henry is the sort of man I could've met through a personal ad in *New York* magazine. *Divorced white male, 40-ish, father of two children plus cat, hamster, and goldfish.*

Solvent, kind, good-looking, and fun-loving, but is not afraid to cry.
Likes music, movies, long walks on the beach, and YOU?

I return the photograph to Henry, and I ask him, "Do you still love her?"

A flicker of doubt crosses his face, and I catch it there. Still, he says, "Definitely not. No way." Glancing once more at the picture of his ex-wife, Henry is reminded that, except during the summer months, she did not shave her legs or underarms, spots where also her hair grew like shrubbery. He next tells me how, in lieu of a proper blow job, she acquiesced only to something like playing the harmonica, her lips pursed along the shaft. Not once in the entirety of the twelve years they were married did she take the whole of Henry's cock into her mouth. "And get this," Henry says. "Every year for my birthday, she gave me a chamois-cloth shirt mail-ordered from L.L. Bean. Except one year I got a book on dolphins. Dolphins are nice," Henry says, "but it's not like I was interested in them." Then he asks, "What about you?"

"Me?" I say. "I take it in my mouth."

Henry laughs, but also he is blushing like a tea rose. "No. I mean, have you ever been married?"

I nod, and I say, "Yes. Once. Briefly."

"So you're divorced too." Henry thinks we have that in common, but I tell him, "No. I'm a widow."

"Oh, I'm sorry." Henry is flustered. As if he's made a social gaffe, he fumbles with words and gestures. Like a pair of trout on land, his hands flip against the air and slap his face and the tabletop. "Really. Sorry. Oh, I shouldn't have said anything. Would you like more wine? Let me get you another glass of wine."

We, Henry and I, did not meet through a personal ad because— for what it's worth—when it comes to men, I have never experienced deprivation or even slim pickings. It could be that I am heavy with pheromones. That I give off an irresistible stink. Or maybe men go for me because they like a toothache, because in all modesty, I'm not always the easiest person to get on with. Whatever. Also, it doesn't hurt any that I have a certain celebrity, albeit minor, but that does come with a kind of cachet.

Bent on getting me another glass of wine, Henry raises his arm to signal the waitress. I reach across the table and take his hand. "Henry," I tell him, "my glass is full."

No matter or not that I am popular with the men, I would never have answered such a personal ad because while I like cats and music well enough, I'm not keen on the movies. Or children, and spare me from long walks on the beach. The beach is an area I actively dislike, and men who cry are not for me. I do not have what it takes to care for the emotionally enfeebled. I've got my own problems.

Leaning in to diminish the distance between us, as if nosing about in my business requires physical intimacy, Henry asks how it happened. "How did he die?" His voice is soft and it comes from the back of his throat. It is not necessary to look or to touch to know that, as we speak, Henry's pecker is growing stiff like rigor mortis has set in. It's this situation about me being a widow that's doing it. As if all women widowed young are like spiders. Black widows. Seductively mysterious and titillating and dangerous. A femme fatale, and perhaps for real. As if maybe I am capable of bringing on killer orgasms. Henry is not the first man of my acquaintance to burst his fly over the possibilities. "Your husband?" he presses for an answer. "Was it an accident?"

"Complications." I tell him that much. "He died from complications," I say, and then I leave it alone. I do not explain what is meant by complications. Entanglements. The raveled skein of yarn that is story's tragic element, the labyrinthian free falls of choice, the momentum of things out of control, of fear and human failings. Better he should think Max died from a bowel nicked during a routine appendectomy. Or from pneumonia. The tragic conclusion of a common cold neglected.

I bill myself as a widow, I refer to Max as my dearly departed, I incant may-he-rest-in-peace because this is one of those cases when a falsehood embodies a greater truth. A metaphorical truth because the literal truth would serve only to distort the picture of my marriage to Max. As if our marriage were simply yet one more marriage that didn't pan out. As if we were but a statistic in the annals of divorce. A marriage gone belly-up due to squabbles over money or that he ran around on her or that she grew fat or that they grew apart. All the usual reasons for a marriage to go kaput. Our marriage was not that way. Not at all.

To do my marriage justice, a death was required. Death was the way it had to end, the only exit available, and Max had to be the one to take it because it wouldn't be logical for me to be the dead one. Despite that there is more than a shred of evidence to justify the statement, "My marriage ended because I died," I could hardly say such a thing now and be believed. Not while I'm sitting here window-side in a trendy downtown tavern with my hand under the table and resting on Henry's leg. My fingertips make small and soft circles around his knee. Circles of intent, and not to mention I prefer the part of the widow to that of the corpse.

In this version of the story, the part of the widow is a small one. There was no scene where I stood graveside weeping while a casket, with Max in it, was lowered into the ground. No mass was said for Max, and I did not write an elegy for his memorial service either. That's because there was no memorial service. I did not sit *shiva* for him, and I have never left a spray of red roses laced with baby's breath at his headstone. Indeed, there is no headstone that sports three lines, like a tercet chiseled into marble, Max Schirmer / Loving Husband / 1993–1994, because Max is not dead in that way.

In the conventional sense of the word, as far as I know Max is not the least bit dead. Nonetheless, for purposes of my own, Max is as dead as a doornail. A conceit aided along by the fact that he now resides in Los Angeles. The city of angels, which is a place of clear skies, fluffy white clouds, movie stars, palm trees, blue swimming pools, and not at all unlike an afterlife.

Meanwhile, poor Henry here is having something like an asthma attack. His breath is short and rapid, which is a cryptogram for horny as a toad. Considering as how I am responsible for this condition, what with the way my fingers are figure-skating along his thigh, I invite myself back to his place. It is not in my nature to tease, and also because it is my way to ask for what I want. "Let's go to your place," I say, because generally speaking, my apartment is off-limits to guests. The ghosts who live there with me, Dora and Estella, they don't take to strangers, and the ghosts, they were there first.

2

carmen: The Latin word usually meant "song" or "lyric"; e.g., Catullus' *Carmina*. Its broadest usage covered prophecies, oracular responses, incantations, triumphant hymns, epitaphs, charms, and even legal formulas. The word seems to connote divine inspiration, the song of the poet as the agent of a god or muse.

NEVER MIND THAT I WAS UP late last night only to sleep in a bed not my own. Or maybe it is because I was up late and sleeping in a bed not my own. Whatever. I am in a very fine mood. I definitely kind of like that Henry. He's cute. He's sweet. He's got potential. Also, this happens to be my favorite day on the academic calendar. Which also happens to be the last day on the academic calendar.

Grinning like a pumpkin all the while as I turn in my grades, pick up my paycheck, and call it quits for three months at least and with any luck, more than that. By luck, I mean money coming in as a windfall.

By profession I am a poet. Unless you equate profession with earning a wage that approximates the minimum. One that allows you to buy something for dinner other than Kraft macaroni and cheese, three for a dollar. For that, for real money to spend, I have been fortunate enough to land the occasional grant or prize to tide me over. Plus I sometimes write book reviews, and part-time I teach.

I teach poetry writing workshops at a small liberal arts college where the admissions requirement is your ability to fork over the steep tuition fees. At this college, there is no pursuit of excellence. Unless excellence means operating in the black. I can't say I'm fond of teaching except for the part about students falling in love with me. Boys, nineteen and twenty years old and cute-as-pie, gaga for me, they make the job worthwhile. Still, despite the obvious rewards, I'd give it up if I could. If volumes of poetry sold like cookbooks and easy-step spiritual guides, if the honoraria I got for readings were nearer to fees paid to disgraced politicians than to chicken feed, I'd tender my resignation in a skinny minute. I prefer having no commitments.

It's a crying shame but this is how it is for poets. We have to have day jobs to survive and to buy the occasional designer outfit. Even famous poets, such as myself.

I am a famous poet, which is but a degree of fame. It's not famous like I get stopped on the street for my autograph, but I am as famous as any poet in America can get without being dead and having an intermediate school named after you. When you get down to it, my fame is downright paltry when compared to that of movie stars, athletes, talk show hosts, and serial killers, but still I was in *People* magazine, which is nothing to sneeze at. A two-page spread in *People*. An interview, a book review, and my photograph beneath the caption "Lila Moscowitz—The New Formalist Makes Waves."

The big to-do over me is that I write strictly, some might say anachronistically, in form. Sonnets, villanelles, canzones, sestinas, that sort of thing, which in and of itself is nothing new, to say the least. It's that while adhering to the form, my language is of the street. Slang and colloquial and foul-mouthed. I write smut and filth in terza rima. My poems are often stark and ugly and leavened with humor that is black. I write of the individual experience in the belief that one life reflects all lives. It is said of me, by those types who go on about such things, that I am a confessional poet as well as a formalist. I suppose this is true, although many of the episodes to which I confess are not necessarily my own. That's how it is with all writers. They steal from your life and do with it as they please.

For a very short while, I dated a fiction writer who wrote a story in which I was a major character. In the story I was a cripple from polio. He gave me matchstick limbs and iron leg braces. "It's metaphor," he said. "For your emotional paralysis." There wasn't a damn thing I could do about that story of his. Other than to compose a villanelle with an uncomplimentary refrain in reference to his anatomy, but that would've been cheap. Instead, I opted to steer clear of writers of all kinds because I am a very private person. Writers, they don't respect your privacy, and that goes triple for me.

Many of the poems I write are about sex. I have a gift for the subject. The ins and outs of it. My poems lean toward the sordid side of the bed, the stuff of soiled sheets. I write about sex because I have no gift for writing about love, and not for lack of trying. I have tried, again and again, but always it's like facing a blank wall that closes in on me, inspiring nothing but panic. Consequently, much of my success is founded on my failure. I am something of a fraud.

This semester it was a boy named Frankie who turned tomato red whenever I neared him. Deliberately, I would stand at his desk, leaning over his shoulder to read what he had written. "Ooooh," I said into his ear. "Nice metaphor. I like them like that. Good. Really, really good." As with all my students, Frankie couldn't write worth a shit. His metaphors and similes were household clichés. *Cold as Arctic air. Hot as the flames of hell. The good girl wears white shoes.* That sort of thing. His thoughts and observations on paper were banal and trite, but I encouraged Frankie because I respected his taste in women. His hankering for me hinted that there was more to Frankie, that there were parts to him uncharted. As if lurking behind the dopey facade was potential for disaster, and I admire that in a boy.

Also this semester, I got a kick from a girl student. One who was as beautiful as she was vacuous. Holding up a pristine copy of *The Sun Also Rises*, she asked me, "Did you ever read this?" Her gum snapping, and she whined magnificently. "I hate reading. I just hate it. I don't understand why I have to read this. What's it going to do for me?"

"Good question," I said, and then I advised her, "Do yourself a favor and don't read it. As far as I can tell, books like that one, they can ruin your life."

I'll miss Frankie a little bit. He is off to be a golf caddie at a country club for the summer months, and I am off with plans to do some work. I have a book of poems that needs putting together. For over three years now, I've been putting together this book. It is to be my third book, but still it falls apart on me. Maybe this summer I'll get it right. Also, I plan to catch up on some reading. Fritter away the afternoons with my friend Carmen. Pursue Henry, and see what comes of him. I've agreed to do a handful of readings, and to speak at a conference in Vermont, and to be part of a panel discussion at another conference in New Jersey. Other than that, I am looking at row after row of unfettered days, which is how I like my life to unfold.

Instead of going directly home, I go to Carmen's place and let myself in. Carmen is in a deep sleep on her couch, which requires a kind of skill because a hailstorm of noise, the steady drill of jackhammers, invades her apartment. It's like being inside a migraine headache here. They are tearing up Hudson Street again. I shut the window, and Carmen stretches and rubs sleep from her eyes.

It's a rite of summer. At the start of the season, men with well-developed biceps arrive on Hudson Street with their jackhammers to break apart the road, create chasms, dig deep holes, and fiddle beneath the earth's surface. At the summer's end, they will lay fresh asphalt and smooth over what they've done. Other than perhaps the fruit of eternal damnation, this ritual seems to be without purpose.

Carmen finished up her semester yesterday. Carmen is an associate professor full-time, if you call wedging three classes into a Tuesday and Thursday schedule a full-time job. Two sections of nineteenth-century American literature and an honors seminar on the literature of obsession. An obsessive streak is a trait Carmen shares with Ahab, Marlow, Humbert Humbert, Gatsby, and Aschenbach. Also, she shares something with the Canadian Mounties. Carmen always gets her man. What she doesn't do is keep him. Carmen has been married and divorced three times. So far, plus she is quite sure she'll be married three or four times more before she's done because that is her fate. Carmen's dissertation was titled "Divine Inevitability: The Numerology of *Lolita*." On Wednesdays, she keeps office hours and attends departmental meetings. She keeps long weekends for herself.

I get comfortable, easing into the armchair, and Carmen goes to the kitchen to put up coffee. Carmen's coffee is dreadful. Bitter and weak and lukewarm. Undrinkable, except that I've grown accustomed to it, and she doesn't seem to know otherwise. Which in and of itself is a curiosity because Carmen is from South America. Paraguay, and even though she came here as a small child, you'd think she'd know a good cup of coffee from a putrid one. I admit I've got a nerve passing judgment on the coffee Carmen makes. Too lazy to be bothered with a filter and all the rigamarole that goes into a brewed pot, I make nothing but instant. Still, my freeze-dried Folgers makes for a richer, more flavorful cup of coffee than Carmen's fresh ground beans. Not to mention that the coffee I make is warmer than room temperature.

Carmen comes back with two mugs of the stuff and sits back down yawning. "I didn't sleep a wink last night. I'm worried sick."

"About what?" I ask, because it could be anything that worries Carmen sick. She worries herself sick about lead dust particles in the air, snipers atop skyscrapers, pesticides on fruit, rapists in the neighborhood, and radiation from the television set.

"You," she says, and she lights up a cigarette. Carmen smokes Pall Malls, unfiltered. "Your birthday. It's coming up and I'm at a loss. I've been racking my brains. You have to help me on this. What do I get you for a birthday gift? What do you want?"

What do I want? If that isn't the eternal question. What does Lila want? "How about love and happiness," I say.

"No peace?" Carmen asks. "Isn't that part of the package?"

Peace is definitely part of the package. Buy two and get one free. If I had love and happiness, surely tranquillity would descend upon my being. I'd be like the Buddha. "Okay," I say, "give me peace, love, and happiness," and then I make a face like I'm retching because I do that. I mock feelings. I sweep sentiment under the rug as if sentiment were dirt. I make jokes to deflect the sorry truths about myself, and I use snide comments to camouflage hurt, and I'm good at it. Well rehearsed. I've had years of practice at feigning imperviousness, and if you fake something long enough, you can come to fool yourself. Even Carmen is sometimes fooled. "No, come on. Really," she says. "What can I get you for your birthday?"

"Carmen," I tell her, "my birthday isn't until September. The end of September."

"Yes. I know that. September. It's coming up."

"But not for four months yet. It's only May. Why are you worrying about September now? And on such a nice day you want to worry about my birthday? It's too early to worry about September. Please wait until August to worry," I say, but Carmen does not agree. "I should have started worrying about it weeks ago. Give me a hint. Something to go on. Books? Clothes? A nice vase?"

I shake my head. I do not want a vase, but mostly I do not want to dwell on my birthday. Already, just this little bit, and an existential woe draws near. I try to shoo it away as if it were a horsefly.

"What do I buy for the woman who has everything?" Carmen asks, and I snort at the notion. "Everything? I am hardly the woman who has everything."

There is much I do not have, and I'm not just talking about the aforementioned big-ticket items like love and happiness, but none of what I lack is a trinket for which Carmen can pay with a credit card and gift-wrap in a box. Still, to help her out here, I mention, "I don't have a vacuum cleaner or a fax machine." I would be a desperate woman without Carmen.

"But you don't want a vacuum cleaner or a fax machine." Carmen knows me. "If you wanted those things, you'd have them already."

It is my way to resist technology until, product by product, I capitulate to it. I was the last person in New York to get an answering machine, but when it broke, you'd have thought it was the drive belt to my heart that snapped, what with the way I carried on. I'm quite certain that eventually I will get myself a fax machine, but not until the last minute. "How about a car? You can buy me a car?" I suggest an alternative gift for myself, which is also a preposterous one. Carmen cannot afford to give cars as gifts.

"Absolutely not." She shakes her head emphatically. "No way. Not with the way you drive. You'd have a wreck inside of a week. I'd worry myself half to death if you had a car at your disposal." Then she pleads with me to help her out here for real. "Come on. Think," she says. "There must be something you want. And what will you want to do? Dinner? A party?"

Carmen will make every effort to get me what it is I most desire because that is the nature of our friendship. We aid and abet and encourage one another to proceed no matter how ill-conceived the venture. I was the maid of honor at all three of Carmen's weddings.

Given how splendidly Carmen and I get along, it's a pity, in its way, that we are magnetically attracted to men. After the abrupt yet entirely predictable demise of her second marriage, I said to her, "We should get married. We'd make for a happy couple," but Carmen said, "I'd never marry you. Why would I marry you? For what? You can't cook. You don't keep a neat house, and chances are you'd cheat on me. And the incest. That would be wrong." Carmen believes that she and I were sisters in our past lives. I don't know about that, but there is no denying the bond, the blend. The minute we met, we were joined together by ties of affection. Now, we are

united by the cement of friendship, of trust, which is thicker than
blood.

Thus, she and I are doomed to a platonic love. Nonetheless, it is
assumed often, and by most everyone we know, that she and I have,
at one time or another, exchanged kisses of passion, that Carmen
has fondled my breasts, that my tongue has explored the tops of her
thighs. People believe what they want to believe. Never mind the
facts.

Carmen is generous to worry about my birthday so far in advance. To want the day to turn out well for me, but that is an impossibility. My birthdays never turn out well for me. Quite the opposite.
The anniversaries of my birth are fraught with disaster. Never do I
get the gift I wanted most. Or I do get the gift I wanted most only to
suffer the epiphany: What made me think I wanted *this?* I equate the
disappointment with the gift with the disappointment of love, and
nothing suits me on that day. The birthday party is either so big that
I get lost and forgotten, or it's small and miserable and better to call
it a depressing convocation of losers rather than a party at all. It rains
if I have plans out of doors, and I suffer and weep copiously. As if my
birthday is designed to be a reenactment of the birth experience
itself, I seem to relive that particular horror. Or some other horror.
In plain English, I wig out. It is a birthday tradition of mine to go
psychotic or schizophrenic or catatonic, depending on the external
stimuli. In a nutshell, my birthday and me, we don't mix.

"We've got the whole summer here before us. I'm sure I'll come
up with something that I want. Don't worry, okay?"

I promise Carmen that I'll give thought to the subject, although
the truth is that I will try to not give thought to the subject. Still, I
will fail. Now that it's out in the open, it will hound me, invading
my daydreams and interrupting my sleep, and the less I try to make
of it, the bigger it will grow.

Carmen says, "Okay," but she doesn't look any too reassured.
"You are a hard woman to please, Lila," she says. Every year in regard to my birthday Carmen says that to me, that I am a hard

woman to please. Now she asks me, "You want some more coffee?"
I peer into the mug and I am surprised to see that it is nearly empty. "Sure," I say. "Why not?" In the final analysis, I'd rather drink lousy coffee than have none at all, and then I tell Carmen all about Henry.

3

explication: Also called formal, structural, or textual analysis; examines poetry for a knowledge of each part and for the relation of these parts to the whole.

AT HOME, I TAKE MY MAIL TO MY desk and here, in print, in my complimentary copy of *Lingua Obscura*, which is a journal of rhetorical grandiloquence for assholes, some other poet has written a diatribe attacking my work. Which is why the editors thought to send me a free copy without my requesting one. So I could read why this poet who goes by the name Ankh has a problem with my poetry. That's it. Ankh. No surname. Ankh, in this day and age, no less. Ankh.

My ghosts are at the kitchen table whispering between themselves. Ghosts, I have learned, do not sleep during daylight hours as one might suppose, and Dora giggles. Laughter that sounds like wind chimes. I ask them to please lower the volume. "I'm trying to read here," I say.

That Ankh is a poet of questionable abilities, not to mention the critical vision of a mole, does not stop her any. She goes for my throat and my soul because of my use of a word that she can barely bring herself to utter. "The word cunt," she claims, "is not in the poet's diction." She does not write *cunt*, but spells it out. c-*-n-t.

I beg to differ. The word *cunt* is in the poet's diction. It's in *my* diction, and I think it is a lovely word. The way I happen to be smitten with the related word *gynecologist*. *Gynecologist* is a word that rolls off my tongue as if it were greased with butter. Also I am very attached to my gynecologist as a person. As I am attached to my therapist, although the word *therapist* I don't care for much. The word *therapist* sticks in my craw and offends my sensibilities. Still, I'm quite fond of both these men, although I prefer it when the gynecologist does the probing.

It is nothing but a coincidence that my therapist's office and my gynecologist's office are located on this same stretch of Waverly Place, although my therapist does not much believe in coincidence.

I see Leon every Tuesday afternoon from 3:00 to 3:50, which is the therapist's idea of an hour. The same way their year is but eleven months long. All therapists do that, truncate time, shave ten minutes from an hour and delete one month from the year. Most often it is August when they disappear. While they're off splashing in the Hamptons or gourmandising in Tuscany, you are left alone to flounder.

Leon's office is dark and somber. Diplomas from Harvard and the University of Chicago and the New York Psychoanalytic Institute hang on walls paneled with rich wood. The bookshelves are heavy mostly with tomes on personality quirks, case studies, psychoanalytic theory, the *Diagnostic and Statistical Manual of Mental Disorders* volumes I–IV. Also Leon has the complete works of Oscar Wilde. Sandwiched between *Freud's Brain* and Jung's *Dreams* are my books, which I gave to him as gifts on the condition that he not stoop so low as to scour them looking for clues relating to my personal life. Also, I refused to scribble a few words plus my autograph on the title pages. "I don't write cheesy messages on title pages," I told Leon, which is not entirely a rule I live by. For strangers, for my students, for an audience, those who show up to readings clutching books in sweaty hands, for them I am delighted to inscribe slop on the title page.

I take my seat, the bull's-eye, dead center in the middle section of the three-piece couch that is semicircled around Leon's chair.

This couch is designed for group therapy. Leon does groups three nights a week. I've not been asked to join one, but even if I were invited, I would refuse. I'm hardly about to share my intimacies with an assortment of victims of life's little disappointments. Still, it would be nice to be asked.

Directly across from me, in an S-shaped Scandinavian chair, Leon sits contorted like a pretzel. I associate those chairs with back troubles and with old hippies whose potbellies and sagging breasts obstruct their view of the Birkenstock sandals on their feet. Leon, however, is sprightly, and on his feet are a pair of navy blue leather pumps with one-inch heels. Ferragamo or maybe Gucci would be my guess. Soft leather and classically styled and a tasteful complement to his beige linen A-line skirt. A gold brooch is pinned to the scalloped collar of his white blouse. My therapist is a drag queen, but understated. I like this about Leon. That he is a librarian of a drag queen. I admire his courage, if not his taste, which is way too dowdy for me. You could say Leon gives drag a bad name, what with his knee-length skirts, tailored jackets, sensible shoes, pageboy hairdo, and pearly pink lipstick. Then again, to be fair, I have never seen him outside his office. Perhaps nights and weekends, he gussies up in sequins and feathers.

Also, Leon is sympathetic. He knows firsthand what it is to put on a face. To try to fool the people and yourself. To have it be that your soul is in constant conflict with your matter. That deep inside you are somebody else altogether. Not to mention how Leon knows what it is like to be an outcast and a black sheep. If anything, next to him, I look normal.

"You have a run in your stocking," I tell him, and Leon folds his hands neatly on his lap and waits for more. It's a technique employed by therapists and the police alike. To sit and wait until you cave in to the pressure of the quiet. You give it up and spill your guts. Leon has a genius for this skill. He can wait with the best of them, and I am weak. I confess. "I have a new boyfriend. One that I like," I add.

Leon is pleased, and try as he might, he can't hide it. Lurking behind that cool and professional demeanor of his is a doting mama type who aches for me to meet a nice guy and settle down, which he believes cannot happen until I recover from Max. As if Max were a sickness that is curable, although Leon does not phrase it that way. He says I need to learn to trust, to trust love.

They never did meet, Leon and Max. I didn't start seeing Leon until after my marriage was done with, but Leon's father was lost to the Nazis and his mother went crazy as a result of too much terror, and despite his training in detachment, I can tell that Leon can't abide a German. He won't admit it in so many words, but he worries that Max has ruined something in me just as the Nazis destroyed his mother's capacity to do much other than shriek into the night. What he says is that Max was merely a symptom of a larger conflict.

"So tell me," Leon asks. "Who's the lucky guy?"

"His name is Henry," I say. "He's divorced with two children and a cat and a hamster and a goldfish. He is independently well off. He's very sweet," I say, and Leon shines like a beacon, guiding me to safety until I add, "Who knows? He might be the one."

Leon does not think that it is healthy to jump the gun. He doesn't so much like looking ahead that way. For Leon, the future is not as illuminating as the past. Between Carmen and Leon, I pretty much have all my verb tenses covered.

"You're practicing safe sex, I trust," he says, and I say, "Leon, he was married for twelve years. I'm his first date in over a decade."

"I don't care," Leon says. "Please, promise me. You'll use condoms."

I look away from Leon and I promise him I'll use condoms, which is a lie, and I check my watch. Sometimes the truncated hour isn't truncated enough. Time remains, and I need a new topic to talk about, and so I say, "I've got a birthday coming."

Leon knows something about me and my disastrous birthdays. Not everything there is to know. I have yet to reveal many of the plum details, but I've been with Leon for more than two years now. Consequently, he's all too familiar with the sad tale of my last birthday. How I was going to treat myself nice, how I went to Saks and bought a scarf that was economically way out of my line. A small fortune I spent on that scarf only to leave it by accident in the taxicab, which soured the remainder of the day for me to the extent that I kicked at the walls of my apartment and howled like a wounded wildebeest until I fell asleep from the exhaustion of it. The year before that I found myself locked into a fetal position from which I was unable to unfurl for eighteen hours, and the year before that one—well, that year I was still married to Max. Which was the most hideous birthday of them all. To date, knock wood.

"Your birthday isn't for a ways off yet," Leon notes. "What makes you think about it now?"

"Carmen." I place the blame squarely on my friend. "Carmen is worried about it."

"And you?" Leon asks. "Are you worried about it?"

"I'm trying to not think about it," I say, "but Carmen is pestering me about a gift. About what I want."

"And do you have any idea what that could be?" Leon asks. "What you want?"

"Nothing," I say. "There's nothing I want," but Leon does not let me off the hook so easily. "If it were all going to work out wonderfully," he says, "if your birthday were going to be the perfect day you've imagined, how would it unfold?"

I tell Leon that I cannot imagine such a thing. It is too far-fetched, and Leon gives me an assignment. "Think about it," he says. "Close your eyes and see what you can come up with. Try to picture a happy birthday for yourself." With my eyes shut, I first see only the darkness, which is a far better thing than what follows. Which is Max.

4

free verse: This misnomer is a contradiction in terms. There are only two modes of language—prose and verse. Either language is metered or it is not metered; it cannot be both simultaneously.

As if there were buried treasure at the end of it, Max and I had my birthday mapped out. It was to be a perfect day. *The* perfect day. Max took off work. A personal absence, because he would never call in sick when he wasn't. A man of a particular kind of honor, that wasn't the sort of lie Max would ever tell. We had breakfast in bed.

From there, from bed, oh-so-delicious, we were going to the Whitney Museum to see the Hopper exhibit, and then off for a late lunch someplace swank. Max made the reservation, but he kept the destination secret. A surprise. Max held that surprises were good things, treats. But Max was German and I am Jewish, and history tells us of the surprises they had in store. Which is also my way of letting it drop that, under certain circumstances, I can be something of an ingrate. It's not that I take pride in being an ingrate. It is not one of my finer qualities, but there is not always an available antidote for what ails us.

I wore a lightweight wool dress, eggshell white, with a matching jacket, and on the way to the subway, I kept my gaze downward, daring to see nothing but pavement and feet and small dogs. Only when we were safely seated on the train and it pulled away from the station did I breathe easily. As if I'd narrowly escaped danger. Danger. For me, the neighborhood where we lived was fraught with danger. Which was very real even if it was all in my head. I looked out from the window expecting to spy the enemy.

Above the din of the old subway car, which did not offer the quiet and smooth ride that the newer cars do, Max said, "I am most anxious to see why it is you think so highly of Hopper's paintings."

I had once written a series of Spencerian sonnets where I attempted to tell the stories Hopper had painted. Sad and sordid stories, all of them, of pathetic and lonely and disaffected people, of deviants and of drunks and of pedophiles, but in the end, I tore up the sonnets and threw them away. Poems about paintings are pretentious, no matter how you slice them. Still, a Hopper painting made me ache on the unknowable places inside. Places where I was sensitive and tender to the touch because Hopper's people are lonely people too. Just by looking at them, you can tell that they are unloved and regardless of the number of figures on the canvas, each of them is a solitary being. As if they exist in an invisible box that cannot be penetrated with love or touch. Inside of themselves, they are numb and without hope.

Max had heretofore seen only reproductions. Prints and off-color plates of *Nighthawks* on calendars, and he considered them dreadful, cheap, and cloying. Max went for the work of the German expressionists. Paul Klee, Franz Marc, Ernst Ludwig Kirchner. That sort of stuff, stuff of the mind, which could not inspire me because it hasn't any smell.

"Well," Max took my hand and squeezed it. "I am looking forward to this experience. I am prepared to have an open mind," he said, which was the sort of lie Max told. Max liked to believe he was open to new ideas, but his opinions were fixed entities and chiseled into stone tablets. Also like the commandments, each of Max's judgments carried the same weight. That he considered capital punishment to be state-sanctioned murder was as grave a matter as his estimation of the Beatles as a third-rate pop group. Max was the sort of person who did the crossword puzzle in ink.

It should have come as no astounding thing then when he stood, like the point of a compass, dead center on the parquet of the second floor of the Whitney and pronounced, "Hideous. These paintings are hideous. Sentimental tripes."

The way all good Germans do things, Max learned English by the rules. With Teutonic rigor, he followed the rules of grammar to their logical conclusions. But English is not a logical language and is riddled with exceptions. Strict adherence to the rules took him where strict adherence to the rules took his people before him. Only so far, and then they hit a glitch. The way a robot short-circuits when confronted with emotion, Max was confounded by idiom, which initially struck me as unbearably adorable. Also, he pluralized words that, albeit logically, should've been plural but were not. Like how he first said *laces*, fingering the trim on my panties. "I love laces," he'd said, and so the next time we were together I wore a merry widow that laced in a crisscross fashion from my hipbones to my breasts. "I wore laces for you," I told him, and then it took some time to divine that he'd meant lace, as in the lace trim on my panties as opposed to the laces that tied the merry widow. Although he was tremendously fond of those too. Laces. Like tripes.

"It's tripe," I said between clenched teeth because he ought not to have passed harsh judgments on my taste and on my longings, as if he were disparaging some part of me, the softest part. As if he were saying that my sadnesses were sentimental tripe. He ought to have let his pronouncements go. For once. For me. For my birthday. "Tripe," I said again.

"Yes. It is tripe. Terrible paintings. Juvenile. I am shocked at you, Lila. Falling for such obvious manipulation. These paintings are not the work of a mature artist. They are like sobbing stories."

"Sob stories," I corrected him, and then as an aside I muttered, "Arrogant bastard can't even speak English."

"What did you say?" he asked, although I knew damn well he'd heard me. Nonetheless, I obliged his request. "Arrogant bastard," I repeated. "You have nothing but disdain for people's feelings."

"Lila, what is your problem? People can disagree on matters of esthetics," Max said.

"What is *my* problem? You don't like the Beatles, and you're asking what is my problem? That's how much of an arrogant bastard you are," I said.

Maybe it was merely a matter of taste, but it seemed to me that I had allowed Max a peek at my most private parts and, rather than admiring the loveliness, he dismissed the beauty and the vulnerability and referred to that part closest to my heart as tripe.

"Fucking arrogant asshole," I said again and again, and in no time flat, there we were going at it. An eclogue debat, of sorts. The poetic form of an argument between lovers set in nature, only we spoke not in octaves. Rather, in staccato prose and on the second floor of the Whitney, which was not a cow pasture but was as quiet as a valley, we cursed each other loudly and with much local color. The way firecrackers go off, until I spotted the security guard striding, with purpose, in our direction. Rather than suffer the embarrassment of an escorted ejection from the Whitney Museum, and on my birthday to boot, I turned and cut loose.

Which was, ultimately, how I wanted it, to be alone and miserable on my birthday. I wanted to be alone and miserable on my birthday because there is something comforting about the familiar, and I wanted it to be Max's fault. I wanted to place the blame for my distress at Max's feet because how else could I work up what was needed to eventually free myself from the bonds of this marriage.

Crossing Central Park I stayed not on the clear and paved pathways, but as if I were making an escape, I scrambled through shrubbery and bramble. My shoes sinking into the wet dirt, I went west to emerge, like a feral child from the edge of the forest, on Central Park West. From there I walked to Columbus Avenue. Past all the tony cafés and up-to-the-minute boutiques, I walked on beyond

96th Street to where the avenue lost its sheen. It's rougher around the fringe up there.

I was hungry. Ravenously hungry. The sort of hunger that gnawed at my stomach and at other organs too, but I would not stop for food. I wanted to go hungry, as if it were a challenge and part of the game I was playing, and I grew tired as if I'd been walking for days instead of hours. As if I were an escaped convict or a refugee on the run.

Grimy from the city air, from the exhaust fumes and the grease rising from fast-food pushcarts, my face was streaked with dirt. There was dirt under my fingernails too, and my shoes were caked with mud, when I descended the three steps to the barber shop. A barber shop. Not a froufrou salon like where I now go, where a beautiful man named Kevin colors my hair Black Cherry, but an old-world barber shop for men. The sort with a red, white, and blue pole out front, and inside two raised leather chairs that seemed better designed for tooth extractions than for haircuts. The place smelled from sweet hair tonic. The barber was an elderly black man with a salt-and-pepper mustache.

I sat in one of the chairs, and I scooped the length of my hair into my fist, as if to put it in a ponytail. "Cut it off," I said. "All of it. As short as possible. A crew cut."

That's what I wanted, for my inside and out to match. I'd been living like a camp victim. I ought to look like a camp victim. Such was my reasoning, screwy as it may have been.

"Aw, Miss." His scissors worked the air nervously like a tic. "You don't want me to do that. You got such pretty hair. Leave it be."

Except I did want him to do that, because I was having birthday psychosis, and I insisted. I promised him that I would not cry. Plus I paid him up front including a hefty tip, and so he shook out the bib and tied it at the nape of my neck.

Although I was unable to look at myself in the mirror as he cut and snipped and shaved, I touched it when he was done. With my fingers splayed and my palm flat, my hair felt like the bristles on a scrub brush. Half-inch stubs standing at attention on my head.

Night came, and under the fluorescent lights, I sat on the orange plastic subway seat, my hands folded on my lap. Like the Jews who were refused asylum around the world and had no choice but to return to Germany and the fate that awaited them, I was going home to Max.

My gaze fixed over the heads of the other passengers to avoid the possibility of eye contact, I read and reread the advertisements for podiatrists, fortune-tellers, dermatologists, and ambulance-chasing lawyers (Dial I-N-J-U-R-Y 1). There were no advertisements for the services I needed. Like the International Red Cross or the Allied Forces or a bail bondsman.

Between the 145th Street station and 168th Street, the unmistakable slither wet between my legs. My period. It had arrived early. Five days ahead of schedule. Usually, I menstruated as predictably as the coming of the new moon, and always I bled lightly on the first day. But not this time around. This time I was bleeding like an artery had been slit or like I'd struck oil.

As the train pulled into my stop, I stood up and twisted around to check out the back of my dress. A deep red stain the size of a silver dollar had spread across the eggshell white wool.

At my birthday's end, I darted across the dark streets, moving with the shadows. Bloodied, and with my head shaved, I returned to Max, which was, I believed, how he wanted me.

5

catachresis: The misapplication of a word, especially in a strained or mixed metaphor or in an applied metaphor. It need not be a ridiculous misapplication as in bad poetry, but may be a deliberate wresting of a term from its normal and proper significance. Sometimes it is deliberately humorous.

WHAT WITH THE CLATTER MY ghosts are making, I can barely hear what Henry is saying. "I'm sorry," I tell him. "Could you speak up? I think we have a bad connection." Dora, the tall one with shapely legs and dark hair, is rummaging through the kitchen cabinets for tea, but I don't keep tea in the cabinets. The tea is in a canister on the counter, and, as she always does, Dora will look there last. Estella is a petite redhead with a full mouth and a sardonic smile. She's in the living room fiddling with the radio. Like she's going to find the all-Charleston station. Estella clings to the past. They both do, and I wonder if I'll be following them. As if they've left Arthur Murray–type footprints for me to learn their ghostly dance. Although they died long before I was born, I know what my ghosts look like because they were my grandmother's sisters, and I've seen photographs of them. If they hadn't died long before I was born, I would've been their favored child. They would have doted on me because they would have recognized a kindred spirit.

"Tomorrow night," Henry shouts into the phone. "Would you like to come over for dinner?"

I tell him yes, that would be nice, and he asks, "Is there something special you'd like me to make for you?"

"No," I say. "I'm not a fussy eater. Whatever you decide is okay by me. Except lentils," I remember. "I don't eat lentils."

"Lentils? No, I wasn't thinking of making lentils. Maybe in the winter, lentil soup is good, but this time of year? Who eats lentils this time of year?"

"No one," I concur. "That's why I don't want them."

Max ate lentils at this time of year and at every other time of year too. Always he had lentils soaking in a pot of water on the stovetop. I never did learn if, in fact, lentils were a German staple the way rice is rooted to the Chinese diet or how pasta is a mooring to the Italian meal. Still, I clung to the notion of lentils as the German equivalent of the potato and the Irish because Max swore by lentils as the perfect food. In one form or another, we had lentils every night for dinner. Lentil soup, lentil stew, lentil burgers, lentil salad, lentil sausage, lentil dip. Also, because lentils are an excellent source of fiber, I was not dissuaded from my belief that Germans are overly interested in a healthy bowel movement.

It was morning, midway into my marriage, when naked but for the mug of coffee I held with both hands, I leaned against the kitchen door frame watching Max. Dressed in what may as well have been his uniform—gray suit, crisp white shirt, blue-and-burgundy striped tie—Max stood at the counter making a sandwich to take for his lunch. Gouda cheese, tomato, and alfalfa sprouts on black bread. For breakfast, Max ate granola mixed with yogurt. Max favored natural foods, which, despite his adamancy to the contrary, did not always add up to healthy food. To Max's way of thinking, refined sugar was crystallized cyanide, poison that if ingested was likely to result in instant death throes, but brown sugar was nature's way of blowing you a kiss. Although not a strict vegetarian, Max was not much of a meat eater, and I held the idea that Max ate the same foods Hitler ate. That meal for meal, their diets were identical.

Max wrapped his sandwich in waxed paper, which was an anachronism. Not since early childhood had I witnessed waxed paper used for wrapping sandwiches, and even then it was considered hopelessly out of date. Americans go with plastic wrap, Ziploc Baggies, or shiny aluminum foil, but Max folded the ends of the waxed paper with sharp creases and precision.

My first year at college, I signed up for German 101. I wanted to learn German because I thought it to be the language of love. Knowing what can be lost in translation, I wanted to read Goethe in the original. Also I wanted no part of the Romance languages. That slithery *mon amour* and *mon petit chou* talk. As if that were sexy and in a heartbeat my panties were going to drop to my ankles because in French you referred to me as a little head of cabbage. As if I'd want to be a head of cabbage in any language. The German professor, a formidable woman with a bosom like a dining room table, instructed that we take out a piece of paper. "Fold it in half," she said, and she goose-stepped up and down the aisles to inspect the folds. Those of us who had not folded the piece of paper exactly in half, corner atop corner and no overflow, were given the boot. "German," she said, "is a precise language. If you do not understand that *half* is a mathematical exactitude, I say you have no place in this class." Along with the other dozen or so slobs, I gathered up my books and registered for French. *Mon petit chou.*

Tearing a banana away from the bunch, Max turned to me and said, "We're down to the rind of the bread." Only he pronounced *rind* with a short *i*, as in *window* and *kindred*, and love rushed over me. "It's rind," I told him. "Long *i*. Rhymes with *kind, find, mind.*"

Max's brow furrowed and exposed his bewilderment. "Are you certain of this?" he asked.

"Quite certain," I said, and then I mentioned, "Also, we refer to that end slice of the bread as the heel. The rind," I said, employing the short *i* to tease him for the fun of it, "is the skin of fruit."

"Oh, English." With a wave of his hand, poof! Max dismissed a language, a 1,500-year-old history and a million or so words.

Years before I knew Max, on a tour of Middle Europe, I visited Heidelberg, where I bought a guidebook that contained a detailed chronology of the city. Beginning with the building of a bridge, every fart and belch got a mention from the year 800 right up until 1933, when there had been some kind of brouhaha at the university. There the chronology stopped, and did not pick up again until 1955, postreconstruction, at the inauguration of the new railway station.

They've got a knack for that, the Germans. Poof! They can dismiss history and words, among other things, with the wave of a hand.

"Well, whatever you call it, this is the last of the bread." Max held up the heel, the deep brown oval slice of crust no bigger than an egg. "Could you pick up a fresh loaf today?"

"No," I said. "I can't. I won't be going out today. Not at all."

It happened in pieces that I wouldn't be going out that day or any other day either. At first, it was because of love. I was in love. Why go out when I was in love? When I could stay in and be naked. When I could luxuriate in the yielding to all desire. I could abdicate responsibilities for the sake of perpetual passion. I quit the world to become an odalisque. It was my choice to remain indoors lounging on the couch or the bed. At least I thought it was my choice, an option I exercised, but when I did, after a time of this, consent to join Max for a walk in the park, I went dizzy there. Not a euphoric and pleasant dizzy, but the sick-feeling kind where your stomach whirls counter to your head, which results in anxiety. Next, I was unable, physically unable, to enter the butcher shop; my hand gripped the door handle but no action followed except to backtrack and go home until, in a matter of days, I could not so much as stick my nose outside the confines of the apartment without suffering from panic. If Max were aware of my agoraphobia, he chose to avoid the subject. Its effects and its causes. Perhaps it was good for him too that I was self-interned because it wasn't often that he asked me to go out. Prior to this request for bread, it had been weeks since he last asked.

Sniffing like a dog on the trail of a scent, Max had looked up from his desk, which was not really a desk but rather a drafting table. Clean and white with an automatic-focus projector beneath high-powered illumination. "There is a bad smell coming from the trash," he noted. "Would you take the garbage to the incinerator?" Max wanted a small favor of me.

My heart went off with a bang. My hands trembled and my knees turned gelatinous. "No," I said.

"And why not?" he asked.

I ran my hand along the stubs that used to be my hair. With my head shaved, never would I go near the incinerator. "Because," I said, "I have work to do."

Just the same as I could not go to the incinerator, I could not go to the bakery that stocked the dark bread to which Max was partial, Kristal's Bakery, and Kristal spooked me. Her black eyeliner whipped into cattails, and her hair was teased into a beehive of ultra-ultra proportions. She spoke in a thick accent that Max identified for me as Bavarian, and had she not been on the far side of sixty, she could have played the part of the villainess in a James Bond flick. However, the fact that she was forty or so years too old for that role meant that she could have had a cameo role, small but memorable, in another film. One based on historical events. Like *Schindler's List* or *Ilse: She-Wolf of the SS*.

"You cannot find ten minutes to spare in which to go to the store?" Max had asked.

"No." I got huffy. "I cannot find ten minutes to spare in which to go to the store. I cannot find ten seconds to spare for any reason. Do you have any idea how much work I have to do today?"

I could not go to the store and I could not go to the incinerator and I could not go to the bank or the library or the post office. I could not go anywhere beyond the walls. I made my excuses, mostly that my refusal to leave the apartment revolved around work. That I was near completion on my book, that I had to find shape for the volume, as a collection should be like a calligramme, which is a poem where the words are arranged to reflect the subject. Such as a poem about a tree that is shaped like a tree. Therefore I could not spare ten minutes to take a walk or to run an errand. I'm talking about the very same book I plan to finish this summer. Then, the same as now, my book was nowhere near completion because I'd quit working on it just as I'd quit going out, and for pretty much the same reasons.

It was better that I remain in hiding. Let Max bring me food and the newspaper.

Max put his inspired-by-Hitler sandwich in his briefcase. That part too—the business of packing a lunch to take to work—struck me as a decidedly German thing to do. Americans grab burgers on the run. Devil-may-care, caution-to-the-wind, we order sandwiches from the deli to be delivered to the office, and we charge high-dollar lunches to the company expense account. We are a wasteful lot because, mostly, we don't know what it is to go without.

Crossing the room to where I stood, Max walked with his feet turned out like a duck. As if he had a beer belly. Which he did not have. He was rail thin. Yet he began to take on the stance of a burgomaster and it seemed to me that he was wearing his trousers hitched higher than his waist. As if he were becoming his forefathers, and also I must ask, what did it say about me that I, a Jew, found this image of Max as townsman of Wiesbaden, if not attractive, then decidedly exciting?

With one hand caressing my bare breast, Max kissed me on the throat. "Do not despair," he said. "I will get the bread," and he left me in a state of want.

At my desk, I stood and leaned over the chair as if someone were sitting there, and I wanted that person to smell my perfume. The pages of my manuscript were spread out in a mess. I was on leave from teaching, without pay because part-timers—even illustrious ones such as myself—get the shaft instead of a sabbatical. It was my intention to get this manuscript into shape. To revise each sonnet, each ode, each aubade, each rondeau word by word, syllable by syl-

BINNIE KIRSHENBAUM   45

lable, until my iambs skipped and my trochees slid home. To polish
my nouns until crisp images were reflected back at me, to push
verbs into activity, and to hone spare adjectives into edges sharp
enough to draw blood. Under other conditions, it was the kind of
work I like best. Amusing myself with language. The challenge of
tinkering with the words while holding true to the form and the
rhyme scheme. Moving and molding and shaping and shaving and
carving until the pieces of the puzzle fit together and with a snap.

However, it is not possible to get a manuscript into shape when
you are falling apart. The words on the page blurred as if it were my
eyes that were failing me.

Surrendering to the ailments both real and not, I turned on the
music and I went to the couch. As I had done the day before and the
day before that and back some more days into weeks, I lay down.
The back of my hand resting on my forehead, I lounged like Camille
in the buff. Aware of little else but the sun as it shifted from morning to noon, when there came a knock on my door. So softly that it
might've been my mind playing tricks on me.

Lowering the volume on the CD player, I slipped on my robe,
and I found a shriveled woman on the welcome mat. She had a face
like crumpled paper and a wicked case of osteoporosis. The sort of
old woman who looked as if she might have a poisoned apple with
my name on it stashed under her cloak.

"I'm sorry to trouble you," she said, "but you were playing the
piano? Brahms?"

"The piano? No. We don't have a piano." Then I realized. "Oh.
It was the CD."

"CB?" she said. "What is CB?"

"CD," I said, and I invited her in to show it to her. She marveled
at it and wondered aloud, "What will they think of next?" and I
stared at the numbers tattooed on her wrist wondering, to myself,
the very same thing.

"Bergen-Belsen." She'd caught me looking. "But never you
mind that. It was a long time ago. Before you were born even."

"Yes," I said, and I felt awful about that. Like I ought to have been there too, that it wasn't fair that at the age when I was sleeping in a canopy bed, she was sleeping in a cattle car, and I apologized to Mrs. Litvak about the music. "I'm sorry I disturbed you. I'll keep the volume down from now on."

"Oh no," she said. "Please. I came here because it was so beautiful. I followed the music. That CV, it makes good sound. Like in a concert. I have not heard such beautiful music in many years."

I went back to the couch and waited for the day to be done with, for Max to come home to me. Waiting naked and hungry and his for the taking because that is what I did with Max. I waited and I thought about the surrender that would come when Max did, and I thought about what it means when the line between enemy and beloved is clearly marked, and is there a word for that, for when you've crossed it?

6

chansons de geste: the term by which the Old French epic poems relating the deeds of Charlemagne and his barons were known. "Geste" has additional senses of history and historical document, and by further extension it comes to mean "family, lineage."

HENRY GIVES ME A GREEN PEPper that is curvy and lascivious, and he says, "Here. Chop this," which is both galling and sexy at once. I'm not sure whether to say, "Chop it yourself, asshole" or else drop to my knees and unzip his fly. The indecision results in a kind of freeze, where I'm stuck between two places. Also, if you invite me to dinner, I don't think I should have to do any of the cooking.

In a salad bowl on the countertop, Henry's goldfish dances in the water. Its hindquarters wiggle and its tail looks like something Esther Williams did in a pool. "Your fish dances," I remark, and Henry says, "Yes. That means he's hungry." Henry goes to the cabinet for fish-food flakes, which he sprinkles into the water. Then, he says to me, "The knives are in that drawer there." With a cock of his head, Henry indicates the one to my left.

I am perfectly well aware that it is the wrong tool for the job, but still I take out a butter knife and squint at the fine print. Reed and Barton. Henry has sterling flatware from Reed and Barton.

Fancy that. Fancy-schmancy that. Very fancy-schmancy that.

Nosy thing that I am, I rummage through the drawer to see what else he's got there. I come up with a stack of what appears to be six miniature gravy boats. Also sterling and monogrammed. "What is the purpose of these?" I ask.

"They're for almonds," Henry tells me. The little gravy boats are for almonds. Each place setting gets an individual serving of almonds so that there is no reaching into a bowl like pigs at the trough. An elegant concept, but the bowls are so small that you could fit no more than five or six nuts, tops, in each one, which is a chintzy portion. Especially if the almonds are salted.

If my mother were alive, she'd be peeing in her pants over Henry here and his Anglo-Saxon ways, that washed-out oh-so-pale blue blood coursing through his veins, his Reed and Barton flatware. Her hope for me on this earth was that I'd stumble up the social ladder and into the land of lime green and pink. But the dead cannot pee in their pants, and I consider these almond boats an embarrassment.

Henry's bachelor pad is crammed with the effects of money minted generations ago. Silver candelabra and tea sets, lead crystal vases, Limoges battersea boxes, linen tablecloths. The stuff of a dowager. Old-lady *tchotchkes.* Generally speaking, recently divorced men have all of two bowls and a spoon they picked up at Pottery Barn. Henry has Wedgwood. Service for twenty-four, including the soup tureen.

As if that's not sufficiently peculiar, hanging on the wall in his foyer is a letter from then President Eisenhower. Matted in ecru and framed in no-nonsense black. Eisenhower had written to Henry's parents congratulating them on the birth of their son. In reference to Henry, the president wrote, "It is with great joy that I welcome the littlest Republican into the world."

When I first saw that letter, I asked, "You're a Republican?" If my ghosts were to discover that I were boinking a Republican, they'd die all over again. Like me, Dora and Estella breathed left. Often, I hear the pair of them humming the "Internationale." I had to say, "I'll be square with you here, Henry. I'd blow a baboon before I'd suck a Republican dick. That's just how it is with me." Which is quirky of me. How I could do Nazi progeny, but I draw the line at Republican.

Henry swore up and down that he is a registered Democrat. "A liberal Democrat. Very liberal," he promised, but it could be that he was only trying to pass. "It's just that my mother was friendly with the Eisenhowers," he told me. "Mostly with Mamie. They were alumnae of the same finishing school or something. It was a social thing between them. My mother never talked politics. You would've liked my mother," he said.

I doubted that. A chum of Mamie Eisenhower's, and one that never talked politics, no less. I could just see Dora's face at hearing that. No, I would not have liked her. Only I didn't say so because it's bad form to insult a person's mother. Particularly when the mother in question is dead. Henry's mother has been dead for six years, and his father for seven. Yet they are with him, because Henry keeps their ashes in shoes boxes stacked in the hall closet. His mother's mortal remains are in a pink Pappagallo's box, ladies' flats, size nine. His father is in a box from Johnston & Murphy, black cordovan, size ten and a half.

Henry has a reasonable explanation for this grotesque effrontery to the dead. Quite simply, he hasn't gotten around to burying his parents' ashes or sprinkling them as if they were fish food over a body of water, but he plans on it. "One of these days. Soon," he said, and he told me, "It was a very chaotic time in my life when they died."

That's his excuse, but I have ideas of my own as to why Henry's parents are in shoe boxes nestled between his ski boots and a gallon-sized jug of Spray 'n Wash. Ideas that rely on screws loose in his head as the result of the thinning of the blood line. You're always hearing about these kinds of kinks in royal families. Along with hemophilia A and the Hapsburg chin, they are prone to porphyria, which shows itself in behavior that is batty. It's the enrichment of homozygous genes that does it. Inbreeding, which produces dukes with six toes on each foot and poodles that do nothing but quiver and piddle on the carpet.

Each new apple on Henry's family tree put stress on the roots. Subsequent generations found themselves less well off, both in the pocketbook and in the head. Still, because there was a bundle to start out with, Henry might not be filthy rich but he is able to live quite comfortably off his inheritance. Which is a good thing because Henry has no job. "I haven't figured out what I want to be," he told me. "Mostly I like to putter."

Yet Henry refers to me as a princess. "Such a princess," he says. "You are such a princess. You don't even know how to chop a pepper." Apparently, I am not chopping to specifications. "We're making pasta sauce. We want small pieces for flavor." Henry takes hold of a ragged slice of pepper and waggles it as if it were a worm. "These are slices for a crudité." He tsk-tsks my inept handling of the pepper.

Pardon me for not employing proper chopping procedures. For not knowing there was a right way and a wrong way to chop a pepper. I don't know from chopping peppers or making pasta sauce from fresh vegetables because I, too, come from money. Nothing like the sort of money from which Henry sprang forth. Ours was the sort of new money which bought us pasta sauce in jars from Waldbaum's supermarket.

On the boat to America, my paternal grandparents, Papa Moscowitz and Grandma Tessie, then newlyweds, shared their quarters with goats, which was step one to making a better life. My father and his sister Mitzie were born in a tenement in the Bronx where Papa Moscowitz eked out a pathetic living washing windows. *Schlepping* a bucket and rags, he dragged his sorry ass from storefront to storefront asking, "Hey, Mister. You want I should wash your windows today?"

What with all those years of scrubbing pigeon shit off glass, it was enough to quiet any man's dreams. Whatever hope he had left, it was for his children.

While attending the City College of New York, my father took a class in industrial design. There, with the intent of easing his father's burden, he constructed a lightweight, lightning-fast industrial squeegee. Not the least bit taken with the newfangled gizmo, Papa Moscowitz preferred to stay with his rags and develop permanent elbow damage. My father, however, was frothy with first-generation enthusiasm. A man with a vision, pole-vaulting on his industrial squeegee, he launched a seriously profitable window-washing empire.

His sister Mitzie grew up to bleach her hair blond and become a real estate tycoon. She married some *schmuck* and together spawned Howard, who was good with numbers.

With money in his pocket and looks like Tyrone Power the movie star, my father set out to win the affections of Isabelle DiConti, a Botticelli-like Venus whom he'd met at a party where City College men were introduced to Hunter College women. The DiContis were a once hoity-toity Italian-Jewish family who lost every nickel long before my mother was born. My mother and her parents lived on airs alone in an empty apartment on Riverside Drive. "We had no furniture," my mother told me, "but we had a good address." The DiContis didn't always have money for food, but my mother's winter coat was cashmere.

Like the young Jacqueline Bouvier, my mother was more than happy to trade her lineage for an infusion of hearty genes and a wad of cash. With the one small provision, as is so often the way in any fairy tale: a task to be performed. To prove his love, my mother requested that my father change his name because no way was she going to go through life as Bella Moscowitz, which was too too identifiably Jewish. It was okay to be Jewish, but it was not okay to be too too Jewish. As a result, I am Lila Moscowitz, née Morse.

Morse. Like the guy who came up with the code. Morse. As in Inspector Morse, the English detective whose eponymous show we get on our educational television stations.

"So, I Americanized it," my father said, justifying the rejection of his heritage.

"You did no such thing," I argued over the dinner table. "You anglicized it. Moscowitz is a perfectly good American name. Land of the wretched masses yearning to be free and all that crap. *I* am not ashamed of who I am." With the kind of moral indignation that only a teenager such as I was then can muster up, I banged my fist on the table and sent a salad fork flying. "I will not live a lie," I proclaimed, while my brothers rolled their eyes at their loud-mouthed, obnoxious, too too Jewish sister.

If modern medicine could reattach the foreskin the way they are now able to stitch back an arm severed at the elbow or an amputated foot, my brothers would go for the procedure in a skinny minute. The two of them—Robert the oral surgeon and Michael the professor of economics—wound up married to women cut from the same bolt of cloth, which was linen. Tall and thin and flat-chested, fair-haired, skinny-lipped things. In one of those delicious quirks of fate, Michael's wife is named Regan, leaving me no choice but to call Rob's wife Goneril, which irritates her. "My name is Kate," she reminds me. "Kate. Why is that so difficult for you to remember?"

"Because," I tell her, "you are such a Goneril."

Life mirrors art. She *is* such a Goneril. When my mother was alive, Goneril sucked up to her like milk through a straw. Kissy-poo to her face, but behind her back, my sister-in-law dished my mother for filth. The only time Goneril ever called me on the phone, it was to discuss a dilemma she was having in regard to my mother. "Do you think there is some way we can get her to give us money or gift certificates for Christmas this year?" she asked me.

"I doubt it. Why?"

"Because your mother has the worst taste. She gives us ugly things, and then I have to go to the trouble of exchanging everything."

I thought my mother had rather lovely taste. Not my taste, but not questionable. However, that was beside the point. "My mother," I said, "doesn't have to give you anything. You should be grateful.

How good she is to you. I know how good she is to you because I know how jealous I am."

My brothers were determined to marry women who were not Jewish. Instead, they married a pair of Protestants who found their way around Bloomingdale's so fast it could make your head spin.

When I turned eighteen, I changed my name back to what it should have been all along. I forwent the brief and easily spelled Morse as a way to reclaim my heritage. To belong. I became Lila Moscowitz so I could say, "my people," and have it mean something. As with my ghosts, I sought an extended family, to be identifiably Jewish without all the hoopla, because I really could not keep up with the religious requirements. I embraced the European patriarchy, a legacy that amounted to three rubles and weekly pogroms, but mostly I did it because it irked my parents enormously.

My name reclamation remained the skeleton in the family closet until it was splashed over the pages of *People* magazine. No one reads poetry but everyone reads *People*. Even if they deny it, they read it while standing on line at the supermarket or in the dentist's waiting room. "Moscowitz," Bella made excuses to her friends and neighbors. "Oh, that's her pen name. All the writers have pen names. Mark Twain, O. Henry, and Richard Whatever-It-Is is really Stephen King."

"Why do you lie about my name? Our name," I asked her, and she said, "Why do you want to embarrass us?"

They were so far gone, my parents, so in up to their eyeballs with Protestant envy, that when I owned up to the full truth about Max, about how he was a blood relative of Albert Speer, how he was practically Speer's nephew, all my mother said was, "Oh. Well, now I know where Max got his good looks."

We were the sort of Jews who underwent baptism in the blue chlorinated waters of the swimming pool at Fox Hill Country Club. The way rich Romanians bought themselves titles to nobility, my parents bought the rights to an eraser. As if there were no history to contend with, as if nothing had ever happened, my parents considered themselves to be like Adam and Eve dwelling in the paradise of Westchester County. Adam and Eve, who were Jews, but not overtly Jewish. Nothing like Moses. That fanatic. Moses, he was the sort of Jew who disgraced my family, what with all the yelling and the miracles and that beard.

To be Jewish like Moses was un-American. Something for which Joe McCarthy could bring charges against you. Bella held that Jews should be unassuming and irreligious. She had it in big time for the Orthodox and especially for the Hasidim. As if they sullied her with guilt by association. She cursed them for wearing their faith— yarmulkes, beards, payas, tefillin, long black coats in summer yet, wigs and babushkas—for the world to see and to mock. "Filthy and ignorant. They give all Jews a bad name," my mother said.

Not that we newly rich American Jews didn't have our own ritualistic garb. Oh, but we did. Designer clothes with the labels showing. Oscar de la Renta emblazoned across the chest. Gloria Vanderbilt and her swan on the pocket of our jeans. Louis Vuitton pocketbooks, which—I'm sorry but it's true—look like diarrhea-colored vinyl totes that I wouldn't give five dollars for. We frosted our hair and we painted our fingernails with frosted polish. The way the baby Jesus was given gifts of gold, frankincense, and myrrh, I got goodies such as a birthstone ring, an add-a-pearl necklace, and a name necklace—*Lila* scripted in 14k gold, the *i* dotted with a diamond chip. I slept in a canopy bed, a pink princess telephone on the nightstand. I had cashmere sweaters by the yard and a junior fur, which was a jacket made from dead bunny rabbits and something like a training bra in that it was preparation for the mink coat of future womanhood.

If all had gone according to my parents' plan for me, instead of a small and haunted apartment on Morton Street, the ancestral digs, I'd be living in a big and new house in Connecticut, the gateway to New England. I'd be wearing tartan plaids in winter and pastels in the spring. My husband would have the pizazz of a Ken doll and we would have a big dog, a setter or a retriever. Because we would not hunt—not even the most assimilated Jews play with guns—the dog would point toward Greenwich. Somehow, dominant and recessive genes not withstanding, I'd have blue-eyed, blond-haired children, and my grandchildren would wind up like Henry, living off a dwindling trust amid the relics of better days.

Henry takes what is left of the pepper away from me, and he banishes me from the kitchen. "You're useless," he says. "Such a princess. Hopeless."

Henry may have his sterling flatware from Reed and Barton, but I've got hybrid vigor. While he's slaving over a hot stove, I'm in the living room with my feet up on the coffee table. I'm drinking chilled white wine from a crystal goblet. Like the princess I was raised to be.

They raised me to be a Jewish princess, but my parents wanted me to be an Episcopalian. Now Henry, an Episcopalian, wants me to be a Jewish princess, and let me never forget what Max wanted of me.

7

neogongorism: Hispanic ultraism led the young writers of Spain and Spanish America toward a new gongorism in which the attempt to create striking metaphors was intrinsic. García Lorca, quoting Góngora, pointed out that the only thing which could give immortality to a poem was a "chain of images."

SUCH A PRINCESS WAS NOWHERE in evidence during my marriage to Max. Especially during the latter part, when my hair was growing back at odds and ends, sprouting willy-nilly in patches. Cowlicks were random but many. My collarbone protruded at sharp angles and my knees had gone knobby. Dark circles lent my eyes a desperate and hungry look, and my personal hygiene was lacking.

Getting up from the couch because there was a knock at the door, I put on one of Max's cast-off T-shirts, which stopped mid-thigh and hung loose at my neck. I peered through the peephole.

Despite how her face was distorted by the convex glass, I nonetheless recognized Carmen at once. With two hands, palms up, she was balancing a large brown bag spotted with grease. "Fried plantains," she told me. "Sweet ones, and rice and beans and chicken. You need to eat. Look at yourself. And you've got to do something with that hair."

Carmen dished the food out onto plates, and I asked her,

"Where did you get this?" As if rice and beans and fried bananas were miraculous. Like one fish having multiplied into a slew of fish. "At the Dominican take-out place down the block," Carmen told me. "You know, that festive-looking one with all the flags out front." I shook my head. I did not know the place to which she was referring. Moreover, I did not believe in its existence because there could not possibly be anyplace festive in Washington Heights. Never mind the wide, tree-lined avenues or the flowerbeds or smart Art Deco buildings well maintained. Gloom permeated the streets. The mood was perpetually somber. Everyone was sad.

Carmen pulled a chair away from the table for me to sit. "Eat," she insisted.

Using my fingers like a pair of chopsticks, I brought a sweet plantain to my mouth. It tasted so good, and I groaned from the pleasure of it.

"Let me ask you something." Carmen swallowed a forkful of rice and beans. "Do you realize that this neighborhood is mostly Dominican? Dominican. Not German. Not Jewish. The Germans and the Jews, they're dying out here, Lila. The Dominicans have moved in."

I shook my head. Carmen had to be mistaken. I never saw any Dominicans here. All I ever saw was history on the brink of repetition.

"What is happening to you?" Carmen asked. "All around you, Lila, the streets are lined with bodegas selling mangoes and guava, but you see only that one bakery with the stollen in the window. Listen to the sounds of the streets. It's salsa, baby. And merengue, so how is it you're hearing the strains of Wagner? Plus, no offense, but you look like the living dead."

With the back of my hand I wiped away a tear and got up from the table. "Come with me," I said to Carmen. "I want to show you something."

In the living room, where my desk faced the window, I told Carmen to look. "Look," I said, "and tell me what you see."

The living room window faced out over a courtyard, and because the building was U-shaped, directly across the way was Mr. Greenberg's kitchen window.

"I see some old guy wearing a baggy short-sleeved shirt stirring something in a pot," Carmen said. "What of it?"

What of it? All day long and all night too, Mr. Greenberg was there. Standing at his stove and stirring soup in a pot while I tried to sit at my desk and shape a book of poetry. How could I immerse myself in poetry with that in front of me? "That's Mr. Greenberg," I told Carmen. "He was a camp victim. See the numbers tattooed on his arm?"

Carmen leaned in and squinted. "No. I don't see the numbers tattooed on his arm. And neither do you see them. Not unless you've got eagle eyes. Which you don't. You're half blind, Lila. You couldn't see the numbers if they were on your own arm. You're making it up, about the numbers. You don't know that he was a camp victim. You're just imagining that he was."

So maybe I didn't know for sure about Mr. Greenberg's sorrows, and maybe I didn't even know for sure that his name was Mr. Greenberg, but those are details. The building where I lived with Max and Mrs. Litvak formally of Bergen-Belsen, it had to be crawling with horrible lives.

Carmen advised that I walk below 181st Street and east of Broadway. There, east of Broadway, I would see no one who wasn't Dominican, and if I moved my desk so that it faced another window, I might get a different world view. "Or, I suppose," she said, "you could always leave here altogether. Leave Max."

For Carmen, to leave a husband was no bigger a thing than a breadbox. For me, the dimensions were too high to scale. "Leave Max?" I shook my head as if that were a notion too preposterous to consider. Except that I had already considered it, and I had concluded it was not possible. I could no more leave Max than I could leave my arm or my pancreas or this earth. An escape? How would such a mission be accomplished? "How could I leave Max?"

Things might have been otherwise for Max and me had we lived elsewhere in another part of the city, had we started out in a new apartment, one that was on neutral territory in a benign part of town instead of living in his apartment in Washington Heights. Or better yet, had we resisted entirely the calling to sleep forever in the same bed, had we kept it casual, loose. If only that had been possible.

Early on into our affair we learned that nights apart caused us severe symptoms of suffering. Aches that aspirin could not alleviate, and sleeplessness that resulted in phone calls after midnight. Phone calls to coo, to say I miss you, I want you, I need you. Phone calls that invariably culminated in phone sex, which was nowhere near as good as the real thing. Which led us to spend all our nights together. Which led us to get married.

My apartment gave Max the creeps because it is small. It is what real estate agents call charming, built in an age when people were short, and it is busy with my accumulations. Not the kinds of accumulations that Henry owns. Other than a toy monkey and my ghosts, I have no family heirlooms, but books have spilled out from their cases and are stacked on the floor. Scraps of paper, notes I've jotted down so as to not forget, are taped to the walls and are also underfoot, and because no one can escape their past entirely, I've got clothes, shoes, and accessories befitting my origins. An abundance of frippery without adequate closet space. Scarves are draped over chair backs and pocketbooks hang from the handlebars of my exercise bicycle. I live in anarchy. A state of dishevelment, and the one night he spent in my apartment, Max hyperventilated, which he said was due to the lack of airspace. He needed to breathe into a paper bag.

The lack of airspace, that was Max's explanation. I believed his wheezing fit was the result of meddling by the ghosts. My phantom aunts do not take to company in general and to Max, no way, no how. Devout Loyalists, Dora and Estella never forgave the Germans for that business with Franco. Not to mention the subject of fascists in general and although they were already dead for the Second

World War, that hasn't stopped them from having a strong visceral response to the events that took place.

When he was able to breathe on his own again, Max said to me, "Clutter. It is the clutter here." He shivered, which was a sure sign that my aunts were near, and he went on to document the contents of his childhood home. "We had big, heavy furnitures," he said.

"Furniture," I corrected him. "It's a collective singular."

"Furniture. Yes. Tables and chairs carved with curlicues and gargoyle heads. Every window had velvet draperies to keep away the sunlight, and the vases and candy dishes and figurines, they were everywhere assaulting the eyes."

"Dresden?" I asked, and Max went jumpy. "Dresden?" he said. "What about Dresden?"

"The vases and the figurines," I asked. "Were they Dresden china? Made in Dresden before the war?"

"I do not know about that," Max said, "and nor do I care. All I know is that it was hideous. German and ugly."

It would take a particular breed of masochist to go through the hellfires of apartment hunting in New York City when the apartment Max lived in was spacious enough for a family of seven. With hallways like bowling alleys leading to near-palatial rooms with high ceilings. Barren rooms painted crisp white and empty but for the necessities. A bed, a desk, a couch, a table with four chairs, a bookshelf. All of it was of blond wood and clean lines and new. Max could not abide furniture that was busy with color or shape or texture, and forget about the stuff of little treasures. Max had deluded himself into thinking that his minimal furnishings with the sleek designs and his stark walls were a rejection of his heritage. As if Bauhaus were something the Egyptians came up with. Still Max clung to the belief that by leaving behind German soil and overstuffed armchairs, he had freed himself from all of it. The priggishness, the arrogance, the stiff-necked pride, the need for order, the guilt.

Which was absurd. Never mind that he left Germany. Look

where he settled. Washington Heights where the old people spoke his language and the bakery cases displayed loaves of stollen, strudel, and dark breads. The fact is, no matter how many oceans you cross, there is no escaping whence you came. It is there, with you, always. Like an aura or a bad dream or like a meal that repeats on you, bringing up reminiscent tastes and objectionable vapors.

The past runs not in a linear direction. It is nothing like north to south or longitude and latitude off into infinity. It cannot be followed directly from point A to point B. It shares no traits with the lines with which Max worked, and it cannot be measured in kilometers or miles. Rather, the past is a series of spiralled circles. A spring coiled end to end so that you often bite yourself on the ass, which was something Max failed to understand.

I was not willing to relinquish my Morton Street apartment, because it is like my DNA or the shape of my mouth. It is family lineage. Mine, the way my nose is mine, but first it was my father's and his father's nose. The apartment on Morton Street is, in the same way, mine too. An inheritance of a sort. How many people sign a lease only to discover later that this was the very same apartment on Morton Street where their two great-aunts once lived? Where they painted and played the piano and drank bootleg gin and where Dora embroidered silk handkerchiefs with purple thread. Where, one winter night, they coughed up blood into those very same handkerchiefs.

Max got huffy over my refusal to let my apartment go. "If you live with me," he said, "why would you need to keep a place of your own?"

I must have known. Somehow, all along I must have known that I wasn't going to stay married to Max for eternity. That the restrictions of our life together would close in on me. That love such as ours, by its very nature, has to be fleeting. That when you give up yourself entirely, you've given yourself reason to leave, because, of course, technically, Max was right. If I lived with him, there was no purpose to keeping my apartment, but I held on. I would not give it up. "First of all," I told him, "we're talking about a rent-stabilized apartment in the Village. Nobody gives up a rent-stabilized apartment in the Village. I'm sitting on a gold mine here."

"So then you will sublet the apartment," he concluded with what was a sensible solution.

"No," I told him. "That's not possible. Dora and Estella don't take to strangers."

"Ghosts," Max snorted. "Lila, you are much too intelligent for such foolishness as ghosts."

Maybe I am too intelligent for such foolishness as ghosts, but I know that Dora and Estella live with me just as I know God is there. Faith and need have no relationship to intelligence. Not to mention, I got a whole new set of ghosts to contend with. Washington Heights ghosts, who were nowhere near as delightful as Dora and Estella, and I never did tell Max that my things—my furniture, my dishes, my treasures, most of my books and my clothes—were not in storage as we had come to agree. I'd left everything just as it was, and during the time Max and I were married, I did not sublet the apartment on Morton Street. Instead, for every month that I lived with him, I paid the rent for a place which, unless you count Dora and Estella as tenants, was vacant until after I left Max. Then I slipped back inside, home, as if I'd been away for only a week or two instead of for the duration of a marriage. As if I'd gone to one of those vacation spots which sound idyllic—Antigua or Aruba—only to discover I was there for the hurricane season.

Leave Max, I wondered. I looked at Carmen quizzically and with hope. Was it possible? Could I simply walk away from what was so strong, so overpowering? How does one walk away when one's knees are perpetually weak, and would I survive it? If I stayed where I was, if I remained married to Max, surely I would cease to exist. But if I left him, I might not recover from the trauma. It was as if Max and I were Siamese twins, the two sides to the coin, and he was heads. The dominant force, the controlling one, but I needed his heart to pump blood through my veins.

I imagined walking away fast from here. I imagined it would be in winter, and I would be shot in the back and my blood would congeal on the snow.

"The way you're going," Carmen said, "it's only a matter of time before I find you chained naked to the radiator, licking jelly from a broken jar on the floor."

I hung my head in shame, knowing I was so near to that picture, and most of all, I'd slapped the handcuffs on myself, and Carmen said, "You're not turning into a Clarence here on me, are you?"

Clarence was Carmen's first husband and practically a gift from God. By day, he traded junk bonds, raking in very big bucks. At night, he liked to scrub toilets and floors with toothbrushes in exchange for verbal abuse and floggings. While an apartment that sparkled was a nice touch to a comfortable life, Carmen was lackadaisical when it came to giving Clarence what he needed. Unenthusiastic about putting down her reading to get up from the couch to administer punishment, Carmen would say to him, "Yeah, yeah, yeah. Consider yourself spanked." What Carmen forgot was that there were plenty of other women out there eager to don rubber dresses and six-inch spiked heels in exchange for an oven that shone and a bathtub that glistened. Women who knew better how to make Clarence happy, and sure enough, one of them, introducing herself as Mistress Vivian, came around to collect Clarence and his belongings. Before he left, Carmen said to him, "Clarence, there's one thing I need to know before you leave me. What is it you use on the grout between the tiles to get it white like that?"

I smirked at my friend and said, "No. I am not turning into a Clarence. I do not get on my knees to clean the inside of the toilet bowl with my tongue."

"The task performed is irrelevant, Lila. A slave is a slave is a slave." The prophet spoke the truth but, as was always the way, no one was much listening to her. "Come on." Carmen took me by the arm. "Come back to the table and eat. The food is getting cold. Have some of the chicken," she said. "It's spicy."

8

---

katauta: A Japanese poetic form of an unrhymed question and answer consisting of three parts arranged in lines of 5-7-7 syllables. The question is based on the *utterance:* a spontaneous, emotive word or phrase. The answer, however, is not logical; it is intuitive.

"WHAT DO YOU MAKE OF THIS?" I hand the Baggie to Leon. It is filled with dust, and it is tied with a blue ribbon, and Leon asks, "What is it?"

"It's a Baggie filled with dust. Henry's dust. From behind his couch," I say, and Leon returns it to me, gingerly, lest Henry's dust get all over Leon's navy blue linen sheath. Other than his watch, a ladies' Piaget, Leon has on no jewelry. His lipstick is a soft pink, the same shade as his fingernails and toenails. On his feet he is wearing strappy white sandals which are portholes to the truth. No woman has feet like that. Size eleven and bony, and the tuft of hair on his big toe makes me hurt for him. I suggest wax or a depilitory cream.

It was in an unabashed gush of sentimentality that Henry presented me with a pile of dust collected from behind his couch. He put the dust into a Baggie and tied a blue ribbon around it into a bow.

"He likes you," Leon says, trying to keep his smile in check.

"Oh, I get it," I say. "The same as in the third grade and a boy

likes you so he pulls your hair and makes you cry. I suppose it's a
way to show affection, but what's wrong with a box of chocolates or
a small bauble in fourteen karat gold?"

Leon shakes his head. "Lila," he says, "I'm surprised at you."
His hair swings the way I wish mine would, but I'd have to spend
twenty minutes with a blow-dryer to get it to do that. "A poet of
your stature, and you see nothing in the gift of dust."

"What?" I say. "That he's giving me little microscopic dried bits
of himself? Cells that flake off and get carted away by dust mites?
Yeah, okay," I concede. "That is kind of romantic in its way. I told
you he is sweet."

"You see no other symbolism?" Leon prods, and I say, "What is
this here? Literature one-oh-one? Yeah, ashes to ashes, dust to dust,
what's a bra without a bust, and all that eternal rot," and I can't help
but cast a glance at Leon's bust, which I assume is all padding.
"Sorry," I say. "I didn't mean you. It was just a childhood rhyme
that sprung to mind."

"No offense taken," Leon says, "but let's get back to what you
phrase so eloquently as eternal rot. Eternity. Is it possible that
Henry is attempting to give you a hint of the promise of something
eternal with this dust?"

Something eternal. The way Dora and Estella have a kind of eternal life, and did some young man of theirs present them with a bag
of dust? Is dust collected from behind the couch something like fairy
dust? Is that how it came to be that my ghosts, having died in 1938
within days of one another, simply returned to their apartment to,
more or less, resume the life they'd had before their lungs gave out?

I would like to think so, that Henry's dust will bring me a sort of
immortality, but despite living all these years with a pair of ghosts, I
don't really believe in that sort of thing. With Dora and Estella and
Max too, in a way, as the obvious exceptions, we grow old and then
we die and that is it.

"Would you like to be immortal?" Leon asks. Like maybe that is
a possibility.

"Definitely," I say. "Provided I don't age much, if at all. If I could quit having birthdays, I'd go for the deal," which I know perfectly well is a deal with the devil, but it wouldn't be my first.

My neighbor downstairs on Morton Street is as old as civilization. Dora and Estella remember when she moved in. A pretty young thing with a complexion like strawberries and cream, but now Anna Mason's skin is a translucent pink and, in a bright light, you can see her inner workings. She wears a black cape fastened with a cameo brooch, and even in torrential rainstorms, she rides her bicycle to and from the market. Her steel gray hair, long to her waist, whips behind her as she pedals against the wind. Anna never has a kind word for anyone, and she is as dotty as a bouclé weave. I once considered her a role model, the sort of old woman I'd hoped I'd become, but I've changed my mind. I do not want to be any kind of an old woman.

Leon is finding all of this very significant, and he is practically jumping out of his seat. He wants me to braid together the threads of my mother's illness and death, my dismal birthdays, and my difficulties with love. Not to mention the delays with my book, how it seems as if it will take eternity to finish it. As if none of these lines were parallel, but rather intersecting themes. Themes that Leon returns to over and over again given the slightest opportunity. "What do you see, Lila? Do you see that you don't want to grow old or become ill? You weep on your birthdays, a day that represents both your birth, a babe in your mother's arms, and your mortality. You don't work on your book as if you want to stay in one place. Do you see, Lila?"

I look over at the clock on the shelf. "I see that our time is up for today, but don't feel bad," I tease Leon. "We've got eternity to deal with this."

9

cynghanedd draws: An exact correspondence between the consonants in the first half of the line and those in the second. Every consonant in the first finds its consonantal echo, except that there is an island in the center of the line in which the consonants are in isolation and are not echoed elsewhere.

ONLY AFTER I GOT THERE DID I remember the rule about never going to a dinner party empty-handed, and while the cancer ward was not exactly a dining room, I knew perfectly well that the fiat applied. Not to mention this was my mother laid up in the hospital. It's the wise Greek who brings an offering to the goddess.

Backtracking to the elevator and down again to the lobby, I asked directions to the gift shop, which was down the hall on my left.

I passed over the rows of flowers in green canisters. Carnations bundled together, garnished with sprigs of baby's breath and wrapped in cellophane. It is wicked, I think, to bring flowers to people who are dying. Like first of all you are rushing the funeral. Not to mention rubbing their noses in the fragility of life. A brutal reminder of how something dewy and fresh turns brown at the edges, to wilt and drop dead right before your eyes. How the scent of the perfume turns to the stench of rot all in a matter of days. The dying do not need to have that in a vase on their nightstands.

It was a curiosity how many of the doodads for sale in the hospital gift shop had to do with golf and bowling. A ceramic caricature figurine of a man in knickers sitting atop a golf tee. A pint-sized golf bag with plastic clubs intended for stirring highballs. A pen and pencil set that was a miniature bowling alley with tiny wooden pins and marbles as bowling balls. The pen and pencil rested in the gutter lanes. Presumably these were enormously popular gifts for men having hernia operations.

On the shelf beside the foot-long chocolate cigars—pink bands announcing "It's a Girl!" and blue for "It's a Boy!"—were coffee mugs featuring cartoons of buxom nurses wielding outsized hypodermic needles aimed at bare butts.

Such an array of crap like you never saw in your life. None of it reflected Bella's tastes. I was in a bind over what to do here, and forget about the thought being the thing that counts. That was the sort of pabulum my mother liked to spew from one side of her mouth. It's the thought that counts, and then from the other side of her mouth she railed over receiving a candy dish shaped like a swan and what kind of person would buy such a thing for her. "Like your Aunt Mitzie. She doesn't think before she buys a gift either. Remember, Lila, that space-age tea kettle? My whole house is filled with early American antiques and that idiot buys me a stainless steel tea kettle with a way-out handle. You know she grabbed the first kettle on the shelf. I ask you, Lila, how long would it have taken her to find a copper tea kettle that would have matched my kitchen?"

With profound relief, I spied a teddy bear on a top shelf. A cocoa-brown bear dressed in a calico frock. A girl bear. It had a string of faux pearls around its neck and a pink bow glued to the top of its head, Minnie Mouse style.

It's reasonable to think a teddy bear is an asinine gift for a woman of mature years, but my mother not only was capable of, but prone to, showering inanimate objects with affection. Especially if they were cute inanimate objects that she could dress up in adorable outfits.

Holding the bear by one paw so that it dangled alongside me, like maybe we weren't really together, I caught the elevator just as the door was about to close. There was hardly room for me and the bear what with the way the elevator was filled to capacity with doctors and nurses and a gaggle of candy stripers. Pimple-faced teenage girls in red-and-white striped uniforms who were there because they had nothing else to do in the way of a social life other than to volunteer services no one wanted. Such as passing out tattered copies of last month's magazines and reading aloud to people who desired only to be left the hell alone so they could die in peace.

I pressed 5 on the panel of elevator buttons, and as if they were ashamed, the doctors and nurses averted their gaze. They knew the fifth floor, and that there was nothing left to be done.

After a wrong turn, which led me to a stairwell, I found Room 527. The door was open, and the pageant of floral arrangements, fruit baskets, plants, and balloons gathered into bunches blazoned forth. Such tribute to my mother. You'd think it was the pope whose uterine cancer had spread all over, what with these gifts. Bella had that sort of popularity where people felt compelled to genuflect before her even if they didn't much like her.

Except for me. Try as I might, and I did try—witness the teddy bear—I was unable to get all the way down on my knees. Somewhere between the conception of the gesture and its completion, my joints would lock in a kind of arthritic paralysis. Even when I knew it would win me points with her, I could not kneel. Like when I published my first book of poems. Bella read only so far as the dedication page. "Carmen?" she said. "You dedicated the book to Carmen? I'm your mother."

"Yes," I said, "but Carmen believed in me. She had faith in me, and you did not." Not to mention that Carmen loves me, and this could not be said in truth of my mother.

"It's that I never thought you would succeed," my mother said. "A poet isn't exactly a realistic thing to be." Her lack of faith in me was not, to her way of thinking, a justifiable excuse for my not sucking up. Bella and I went into stalemate. She never forgave me. Not for any of it. And certainly I have not yet begun to forgive her either.

After the end of my marriage to Max, I called my parents to let them know that I could, once again, be reached at my Morton Street apartment. My mother made no attempt to disguise her disappointment. In me. "It's because you're selfish, Lila. You don't understand compromise. You don't know how to give of yourself," she said, which, when you look at what went on during the time of my marriage to Max, was so wrong a statement that I could not begin to correct it.

At the threshold of Room 527, I looked in. My father was seated at the near edge of the bed, holding his wife in his arms. He was kissing her. Not friendly little kisses nor tender either. Torrid kisses. Passionate kisses. My parents were having a make-out session. "My darling love," my father said. "My love. I love you. I love you more than life itself. I love you." Neither of my parents noticed I was there.

I was a voyeur holding hands with a teddy bear. I stayed where I was and watched what had nothing to do with me. I stayed put, a witness to their love, and I swallowed down hard against the bile that was the urge to scream. It was frightening, how their love for each other cut into me. How I cursed them silently. I said fuck you both for loving each other so completely that there wasn't one droplet of love left over for me. I said fuck you, it's your fault. You made it so that there would be no one with me on my deathbed. No one to kiss my dried and cracked lips just the same as if they were plump and juicy and red.

It wasn't possible for me to watch this display of love for another minute more without erupting in anguish. Without howling in pain that was like a slow burn. Without hurling the teddy bear at their heads. Such was the pity of having left puberty behind, that I could no longer throw a tantrum without revealing myself to be utterly pathetic.

I bent over and propped the bear up against the doorjamb, as if the angels had left it there for my mother, and I went to the waiting room.

On a yellow chair, I sat and I wept for the last time. I wept not for my mother who was dying, but for myself. I wept for what I did not have and would never get. On the fifth floor it was not uncommon to weep in the waiting room. Everyone did it, and it was assumed I was crying over issues of love and loss. Which I was, although not necessarily in that order.

10

---

epirrhema: (Greek "that said afterwards"). Composed usually in trochaic tetrameters, it is the speech delivered to the audience by the leader of one half of the chorus after an ode had been sung by that half of the chorus; its content was satire, advice, or exhortation.

A BLUE-AND-WHITE STRIPED PATIO umbrella blocks the sunlight. The umbrella is a must for me, and I agreed to lunch at a sidewalk café on that condition, that I not be exposed to the rays of the sun. I have grave concerns regarding the sun and how it brings on freckles and wrinkles and melanoma. Concerns that Carmen, shrouded in worries of her own, does not share. She's been spending most of her days at the beach, where she browns herself as if she were a roast. Already she is medium rare. I plead with her to wear sunscreen, but Carmen insists her heritage guarantees her immunity from the sun's ill effects.

The ill effects of the sun are not all that Carmen's heritage protects her from. No less than if she'd been raised by a herd of elephants, Carmen is descended from a matriarchy. Mothers, grandmothers, aunts, girl cousins, nieces banding together to run the show. Men come and go, just as they came and went for generations, with little notice or fanfare. In the microcosm of society that is Carmen's family, men are worthless and sorry creatures, which sometimes obligates the women to watch over them. Like the way you have to protect infants and imbeciles and water your plants. In Carmen's world men can get underfoot, but never can they break you.

Carmen wants to talk to me about my posterity, about how my papers and letters need to be collected and filed away for future reference, for graduate students writing dissertations. I put my finger to my lips and cock my head toward my left. I don't want to talk business because I'm eavesdropping on the conversation at the next table. Together then, Carmen and I listen in on the pair of girls who are barely into their twenties and consequently all atwitter and exuberant and breathless over nothing. "So like then he like smiled at me, and like I nearly died right there on the spot," the blond pixie says, and the other one, a cutie-pie in her own right, asks, "Yeah? So what'd you do then? I mean, like after you died?"

I turn back to Carmen and I tell her, "I don't remember what it was like to be that young," to which Carmen says, "You don't remember it because you never were that young."

What Carmen means is that I was never a bubblehead, and before I stop to think about what it is I am saying, I ask, "Are you implying that I never nearly died because a cute boy smiled at me?"

Carmen has the decency to keep mum. She takes a bite of her omelette and does not mention Max, and how I was once reduced to a puddle of my former self.

I did nearly die because Max smiled at me, although it was likely to have been a different sort of near-death experience than this girl had. I met Max because I was lost. In more ways than one. On my way to sit jury duty, I emerged from the subway without my bearings or my glasses, which I kept in my purse except on those days when I misplaced them. I looked up at the street signs, but I was able to see clearly only that which was six inches from my face.

Naturally blurry vision served to accentuate the effects of the rush hour. Men and women in gray business suits looked like storm clouds gathering as they converged. Bumper-to-bumper traffic melded so that it was impossible for me to determine where the yellow taxi ended and the white stretch limo began. Across the street, like a battalion of spinning tops, children dressed in bright colors were disgorged from a school bus. I could find no solid lines save for the buildings and one man standing perfectly still.

His feet were rooted to the pavement as if he were a constant, and he held a clipboard positioned for writing. He was tall and lanky, the way I like my men formed. Plus, he had a nice neck. A very nice neck. I go for a nice neck, to kiss the hollows, to suckle on the Adam's apple, to run my tongue along the length. The way my tastes are, those no-necked men, the ones with heads plopped squarely on their shoulders like snowmen, they leave me cold.

As I neared this man with the nice neck, his face came into focus. His features were decidedly imperfect. A nose too big, and he was slightly exophthalmic. Bug-eyed and beautiful. He had a mouth crafted for kissing.

"Excuse me," I said, and I waited until he looked up from his clipboard. "Could you tell me how to get to the courthouse from here?"

"To which courthouse do you desire to go?" His diction and accent were foreign, but not from anywhere I could pinpoint on the map.

"Oh," I told him, "I don't *desire* to go to any of them, but I *have* to go to the Supreme Court building. At least I think it's Supreme Court." I pulled the crumpled summons from my pocket to double-check. "That's the one. Supreme Court."

"Yes," he said, as if he were agreeing with a conclusion foregone. "For the most expedient route to the Supreme Court building you must follow West Broadway north for one block, approximately seventy-four meters in length. There you will meet Reade Street."

"I must? I will?" I grinned at his word choices.

"Yes." Again, he agreed wholeheartedly, although that was not what the conversation called for. "At Reade Street, you must go east for four blocks. You will cross Church Street, Broadway, Elk Street, and Centre Street, totaling a distance of perhaps four hundred and ninety-seven or ninety-eight meters. At that point you will find that the Supreme Court building is northeast of your position at a sixty-degree angle."

"Thank you," I said, but before I could go anywhere I needed to know, "Which way is north?"

He laughed and pointed, but rather than walking off in the direction of the polestar at night I stayed where I was and asked, "How did you know that?"

"How did I know which way is north?" he asked as if he couldn't quite trust the question.

"No. I mean, how did you come up with those directions? The distance in meters, so exact. The precision and the detail were magnificent. If you go in for that sort of thing."

"Thank you." His head bowed ever so slightly and modestly as if I had applauded him. "It is my job to know these things. I am a cartographer. I work for the Rand McNally company, and it happens that I am currently preparing a derived map of lower Manhattan."

A derived map is one compiled from already existing data and other maps. It is then a matter of the selection process, which landmarks to highlight, any change in street names, adjustments in compromise and order, and choosing a color scheme. Red for avenues, green for parks, yellow for tall buildings, or maybe pink for parks and aqua for avenues. It's the cartographer's call.

Then he smiled, this cartographer. Not a warm smile, but a wicked smile. Like he'd had a nasty, but nonetheless amusing, thought. "Also," he said, "I am German, which could be the better explanation for the meticulous determinations." Tucking the clipboard under his arm, he proffered a hand for me to take. "Max Schirmer," he introduced himself.

One way to assert your Jewishness is to have it in for the Germans. It is a birthright. Ours for the taking. One of the few things to which Jews are entitled.

"Lila." I held on to his hand longer than was polite. "Lila Moscowitz," I said.

So maybe it was that tidbit of information regarding his nationality. The enemy of my people. Did I, the very same Lila who cast off Morse in an ersatz coup to reclaim my Jewish heritage, get the teeniest bit turned on at the thought of doing it with a German? Or maybe it was that smile of his, the way his upper lip curled. Whichever. I was oozing buckets of sap from between my legs. Warm and sticky and sweet to eat and maybe it was desire but maybe it was life leaving me.

Wherever I go and whatever I do, thoughts of Max stalk me. The way Dora and Estella squat in my apartment, refusing to give up what was once theirs, Max is here having lunch with Carmen and me as surely as if he'd pulled up a third chair to the table. Who needs the striped umbrella to block out the sun when I've got memories of Max as thick as the canopy of the Black Forest and just as dark.

As if there were a trail of focaccia bread crumbs for me to find my way back from our table to theirs, I return my attention to the two dopey girls in time to hear the cutie-pie ask the blond pixie, "So? So like are you going to call him or what?"

I tilt backward in my chair so that I'm nearer to their table than to mine. "Don't do it," I break in on their conversation. "Trust me on this. Don't call him. If you nearly died because he smiled at you, imagine what will happen when you kiss."

11

dissonance: The quality of being harsh or inharmonious in rhythm or sound; that which is discordant or inharmonious with what surrounds it. By extension, the term may refer to poetic elements other than sound that are discordant with their immediate context.

As with the french revolution, the transubstantiation, and St. Anthony's Fire, where ergot poisoning results in blackened limbs which fall away from the body like charred stumps, in the end, all of it came down to bread.

On a Friday afternoon, near the close of the winter, there was no evidence yet that spring would ever come. The trees were bare and gray and there were patches of ice on the sidewalk. Max had talked me into going out. Insisted on it, really. To take a walk with him to buy a loaf of bread. "We'll go to the U-ish bakery," he vowed. "Not the other. A rye bread would be nice for a change, don't you agree? Yes, a rye bread with seeds."

With only an hour remaining before sunset, give or take some minutes, Grossberg's bakery was packed like herrings with old Jews bundled up in overcoats and scarves and hats and galoshes. Stooped, hunched over, and clutching their numbers as if, rather than for a place in line, it was a ration card for the bread itself. Some of them looked bewildered, and it was very possible that already there were no rye breads left to be bought.

Max took me by the hand to scout the loaves remaining. We wove our way, in and out through the line of people, to the front of the bakery where the bread was shelved like library books.

Max stood on the tips of his toes to see over the tops of heads, some made taller by fedora hats, when a man tapped Max on the back. His eyes were tired and red and wet with age, and his hand showed the ravages of arthritis and time. "Young fellow," he said. "There is a line here. You must take a number and wait on the line."

I was about to explain to the old man that we were not cutting into the line, that we only wanted to see what breads remained before we took a number, when Max snapped at him, "Mind your own fucking business."

As if I had just discovered I'd been holding a raw kidney, I let go of my husband's hand. Squeezing between the old people who behaved like sheep, I pushed my way out of the bakery.

Max was behind me, and he asked, "Lila? Are you ill? Is there something wrong with you?"

"Is there something wrong with me? No," I said. "There is nothing wrong with me. There is something wrong with you, Max. How could you be so cruel? Have you no compassion?"

"You do not understand," Max told me. "You have no idea what it was like to live in Germany. You do not know how awful it was for me there."

"How awful it was for *you* there?" I said.

"Yes. It was dreadful. All the rules they have. Follow the rules, and everybody was always telling me what to do and how to behave. All the time they have their noses up your business."

"It's noses *in* your business," I said, and Max repeated after me, "Noses in your business. Whatever. I will not allow some old Kraut to give me orders. I left Germany because the climate did not allow for personal freedom. I was sick to death of old Krauts telling me what to do and how and when to do it."

Very slowly and with pointed deliberation, I asked Max, "And why do you think that old man in the bakery left Germany?"

"I do not care if he is U-ish or not," Max said. "A German is a German regardless of religious beliefs."

"Oh yes," I said. "He probably thought that same thing at one time. Only he was mistaken, wasn't he?"

"You cannot understand. You had to have experienced it first-hand." Max spoke with authority.

"All you had to do," I said, "was explain that we just wanted to look at the breads. You didn't have to talk to him like that. He survived the Nazis only to come here, and now in his old age, he gets bullied by some young thug with a German accent."

"My accent is not noticeably German," Max said. "And," he added, "I am hardly a thug, Lila." He should've quit while he was ahead.

"No? Well, you certainly acted like a thug. Didn't it occur to you that you were forcing him to relive the horror? That this little chance encounter with you will haunt him now for who knows how long? He'll have nightmares over this, for sure. He's an old man, Max. Couldn't you have let him live out the rest of his days in peace?"

Max took my arm. "Lila," he said, "you're making mountains out of moguls."

"It's *molehills*," I shouted at him. "Mountains out of molehills. You want to live in America, then learn the fucking language already." I wrenched myself out of his grasp, but somehow I wound up following him along the avenue. When he stopped and entered Kristal's bakery to get a black bread, I waited outside.

Ashamed of my inability to act upon my conscience, that I sought to save myself first, I wanted to find the old man and apologize. To tell him Max meant no harm, that this was just one of those absurdities that Max, a blood relative of Albert Speer, should blame an old Jew for being too German in his ways.

I turned and ran back to the Jewish bakery. Without catching my breath, I pushed at the door, but it did not open for me. Pressing my nose to the glass, I saw that the bakery was empty of breads and of people. They were all gone. How could this be? Gone, and I was the only one who had escaped from Grossberg's bakery. Which perhaps was not a bakery; perhaps the ovens in back were for another purpose.

My feet were cold and damp from the wet air, and the sky went the color of slate as if it were going to snow again. No primary colors painted the landscape. The world, this world, my world, was like a photograph in black-and-white. Or a documentary from before the time of chromatic film.

I walked home, and Max was in the kitchen. "Where were you?" he asked. "Where did you go? I came out with the bread, and you were gone."

"I was not gone," I said. "Not yet gone. I was supposed to be gone, but I got away."

Thus, I was experiencing a kind of survivor's guilt, but what had I survived? A trip to the bakery? Or a year in a marriage that was causing me to asphyxiate myself? Something like a daily dollop of poison or a rationed inhaling of exhaust fumes. Maybe I needed to be talked down from this kind of love the way I could be talked down from a window ledge eight stories up. I went to the bedroom, where I closed the door shut. Thumbing through the yellow pages, I found the number I sought.

On the fourth ring, a man's voice, smooth with caring and moist with concern, recited, "You have reached the suicide hotline. No one can take your call right now, so please leave your name and number and we will get back to you in the order in which your call was received. Really, we will because we care about you," and I had to wonder how many they lost that way. Then, in spite of myself, I laughed, and with that laugh came the strength of the will to survive.

A fox caught in a trap knows it is faced with the choice. It can either wait around to die or it can chew off its own leg, which is a chance to live, even if it means going through life missing a major body part. If I stayed with Max, I would perish. Already I had faded, and I had lost my edges. Having given myself to him so entirely, there wasn't much of me left. I had become hollow inside, an echo chamber. Love had to be forsaken if I were to come through intact.

12

---

asynartete: (Greek "disconnected"). A classical verse composed of independent cola, loosely or not at all connected with each other metrically.

BEFORE, WHEN THERE WAS STILL an option, I had hoped that my father would go before my mother. That he'd be the one to die first. Not that I was wishing for either of them to choke on a chicken bone or to take a tumble headfirst down the stairs. I'm talking strictly a pragmatic consideration here. One of a pair has to be first to die. And after the grieving, when the dust settled, Bella would've fared better on her own than my father.

True, she was flat-out ignorant over matters of finance, knowing to use the credit card for goodies and services but in over her head when it came to paying the bills. And surely my brothers and their greedy rat-eyed wives would've stepped in to rob her blind and swindle me out of any inheritance. Still, Bella was the one who ran the show when it came to making dinner dates, purchasing theater tickets, choosing movies to see. She was the one who entertained, made parties and phone calls, who bought gifts, who sent cards for birthdays, anniversaries, Groundhog Day, Valentine's Day, and for the New Year. My mother set great stock by holidays. Effervescent and substantial as a bubble, Bella would've gone on without my father to have a life diminished, but still one with quality.

My father, the widower now, lives in Florida, in a retirement village where he sits alone in front of the television. His condominium is climate controlled.

Every other Tuesday, I call my father and always it is the same. I say, "Hi, Dad. It's Lila," to which he says nothing, and so I add, "Your daughter."

"Oh. Lila. How are you?" he asks. He is neither happy to hear from me nor the opposite. I am someone about whom his feelings are benign. Not here nor there. I am his daughter, and that is that.

Another thing I used to wish for was that he would be devoted to me. That I would be Daddy's little princess, but I gave up on that one long ago. Right around the same time I wised up to the truth about Santa Claus, the Easter bunny, the tooth fairy, the stuff of extreme gullibility.

"Good," I say. "I'm good. And you?"

"Fine. It's ninety-four degrees outside, but a comfortable seventy-two in here," he tells me. Like that is news. "We're climate controlled." My father now talks as if he were an old man, like his faculties are befuddled, like he has no idea how he got to where he's at. He misses my mother to the point of distraction. The loss has overwhelmed him. Without my mother to love, my father merely exists. Like a single-celled life form, he eats and breathes and excretes, but that's about it. Despite everything, though, he is my father. It hurts to know how lonely he is, and it hurts worse to know I can do nothing to alleviate it.

"You're eating well?" I ask.

"Oh yes. They have wonderful restaurants here." He had wanted to move to Florida years before, for the sun and the sand and the golf and the tennis, but my mother had refused. "Florida," my mother had said, "is the holding pen for death. Everybody in Florida has one foot in the grave, and you wait for your turn to die." It would appear Bella knew of what she spoke.

I then tell my father that I'm glad he's eating well, and I ask if there's anything he needs. If there's anything I can do for him.

"No," he says. "I'm fine."

"Okay then," and there I bring the conversation to a close. "I just wanted to see how you were doing," and I extract the promise from him that he'll call me if he needs anything, although I know he never will. I doubt that he so much as has my phone number written down and he sure as hell doesn't know it by heart.

When I'd learned that my mother was dying, Leon had asked me, "Do you think this will alter your relationship with your father? Do you think it's possible that you might now grow close? Talk to each other beyond the perfunctories? Maybe have a real heart-to-heart conversation?"

"No way." I shook my head at the impossibility of that. It would never happen, and I can't say I wanted it to happen. I would find it awkward and embarrassing and perverted. To suddenly, from out of nowhere with no historical precedent whatever, go and have a personal conversation with my father would seem as if we were kissing mouth-to-mouth. I had come to believe that fathers and daughters ought not to exchange intimacies. Neither saliva nor secrets. It is more comfortable to know exactly what to expect and how our talk will go nowhere.

Readied for the inevitability of the conversation, I wait for my father to answer his phone, which mostly happens between the second and third ring. Only this time, the phone rings but once and instead of my father at the other end, I get his answering machine, which in and of itself is something of a surprise. I did not know my father had an answering machine, that he had any reason to have one. "Hello. I cannot come to the phone because I'm in New York for Bella's unveiling. I'll be back Thursday."

To appropriate a line—something all poets do, only we call it *influence*—it was déjà vu all over again and again.

When I was in the third grade, in gym class, Marjorie Valentine gave a soccer ball a kick with all her weight behind it, which was considerable. Marjorie was big and pink. The ball might've gone clear across the field had I not been standing in its path. I broke its momentum, and it knocked the wind out of me. I mention this now because the sensation is the same.

I'm in New York for Bella's unveiling. I'll be back Thursday. I ought to have built up an immunity to the hurt this causes, the way exposure to a virus can protect you from contracting the disease.

They were always forgetting about me, my family. Forgetting that I existed. Forgetting that I was, at least officially, part of their sphere, and so easily they went along without me.

A typical Morse family outing, the state fair. Something that came around but once a year, and in eager anticipation, I woke at dawn. By the time we sat down for breakfast, for reasons which escape me, I was no longer on speaking terms with any member of my family. All I recall is my mother shaking her head, dismissing what I felt, what was churning and bubbling inside of me as if I were a cauldron of eye of newt. "Come on," she said. "Wash your face. Let's get a move on it. Your brothers are waiting in the car."

"I'm not going," I said, to which Bella said, "Suit yourself."

From my bedroom window, I watched my mother walk the path to the car where my father was already behind the wheel. Gary and Rob were ensconced in the backseat, and I waited for my mother to turn and come back for me, insist that I join them. Instead, she got into the car next to my father and he backed out of the driveway.

Oh, I was on to this game. I knew exactly what they were up to. Trying to put a scare into me, they would drive once around the block before pulling up to the front of the house. My father would toot the horn, and I was expected to dash out the door and hop into the backseat with my brothers. Well, fat chance of that happening. I wasn't going to oblige them so easily. I would not go with them until they apologized and groveled at my feet. Those were my guns and I was going to stick to them, which wound up being moot. They did not drive once around the block and come back for me. They went without me and returned early in the evening, tired and happy. "Never have I had such a good time," my mother declared. "What a delightful day."

Despite the harsh lesson, I never learned that no one comes back for you. When you let them leave without you, they go.

I'm in New York for Bella's unveiling. I'll be back Thursday. When I was little, really little like a toddler, they were always leaving me behind at places. Taking me with them, but forgetting to take me home. The zoo, the supermarket, amusement parks, shopping malls. It got so that I was right at home in the manager's office, where I waited until my parents could be located. Usually, some nice man there, the manager or a security guard, gave me ice cream or candy, and so the experience of being left behind was not entirely an unpleasant one.

After a week in Cape Cod, my family got in the car and my father got all the way to Rhode Island before my parents realized they were short one child.

Because I was accustomed to the abandonment, unfazed I wandered the beach until I found a boy of my own age to play with. After we tired of splashing around in the surf, I coaxed the boy behind a dune to play doctor. My nose was in the kid's butt when they found me. Sniffing butts was the low point of the routine examination but, hey, who said a doctor's job was all glamour?

I'm in New York for Bella's unveiling. I'll be back Thursday. This is a message that asks for trouble. You don't tell would-be thieves that you're out of town. Not if you've got any sense. With my mother dead, my father is a stupid old man, but I can't take time out to worry about that, or any of it now. I've got a date with Henry.

13

....

diminishing metaphor: A type of metaphor which utilizes a deliberate discrepancy of connotation between tenor and vehicle. Its special quality lies in its use of a pejorative vehicle in reference to a tenor of value or desirability. The function seems to thus lie in its forcing on the reader an intellectual reaction. It is a figure especially favored in metaphysical poetry.

"YOU'RE EARLY," HENRY SAYS, but it's not as if he minds. On the contrary, he is pleased. He likes my company even outside of bed. Go figure. Henry thinks I am funny as all get-out, and that beneath the exterior, I am warm and soft. "Like those sourball candies my mother used to keep in a dish on the coffee table," he says. "The ones you had to suck on to get to the gooey center."

I am familiar with those candies. Old-lady candy. No one ever wanted sourballs. Often, they were textured with the lint of neglect.

Henry asks if I want to take a walk before dinner, and we head over to the river, to the expanse of the old West Side Highway, now closed to traffic. A promenade, and at this time of day, it's a circus here. Bicyclists riding no-hands-ma. Dweebs in suits on RollerBlades whipping past. Kids on skateboards doing flips and figure-eights. Lovers of all configurations arm in arm, smooching, dry-humping against the chain-link fence.

Henry and I walk, and when I spy a puppy—a baby mutt with floppy ears, big paws, and break-my-heart brown eyes—I leave Henry to go to it. "She's cute," I say to the puppy's owner, a woman about my own age with cropped hair. She is wearing baggy blue jeans and a T-shirt that reads "Race for the Cure." I crouch before the puppy, going cootchy-coo and the puppy goes wild licking my face. Enough of that, and I turn and see Henry there and he smiles. I stand up and try to look dignified, and Henry says, "You ought to get a dog."

"No," I say. "You have to walk them. On a schedule. And they drool."

Turning right, Henry and I head out to the pier, where we sit at the edge. The sun is low in the sky. The horizon is pink, and we watch the the sun's rays fanning over the water. We are quiet until I ask Henry a question. "Why," I wonder, "don't you scatter your parents' ashes here? In the river. That would be nice, wouldn't it?"

"It's against the law," Henry says, and I glance around in both directions. On all sides, laws are being broken. Flagrantly. Two kids smoking dope. A wino's got his bottle out. Dogs are unleashed. There's public lewdness going on behind us. "Yeah," I say. "That matters."

Henry shrugs. "The river is filthy. It would be disrespectful."

"More disrespectful than keeping them in shoe boxes in your closet?"

"I mean no disrespect by that," Henry says, and I ask him, "But why do you do it? What's the big deal to burying them or scattering them in the ocean or someplace nice?"

"I want them close to me. I like living with them," Henry says, and I say, "But Henry, they're dead."

It's as if he's learning of the deaths of his parents now, for the first time. As if he didn't already know, his chin quivers, his nose twitches and the waterworks are on. "I loved them so much," Henry snivels.

I put my arm around him and draw him near. To my breast, and I stroke his back. "It's okay," I tell him. "You can cry. It's good to cry."

I tell Henry that it is good to cry, but I did not cry over Bella's death, and to the best of my recollection, I have not cried post her death either. Not for any reason. Not when I couldn't write. Not when I ached for Max to the point where I thought my heart was an open sore. Not when all the losses overwhelmed me as if I were enclosed in a bubble of despair.

Henry blubbers and gets snot on my blouse, for which he apologizes profusely. I tell him it's no big deal. "It'll come out in the wash," I say.

It will come out in the wash. Everything comes out in the wash, and so when Henry quiets down to a whimper, I tell him, "They had the unveiling for my mother today. Or maybe it was yesterday."

Sitting up straight, Henry asks, "Unveiling?" Henry does not know from such a thing, and I explain it to him. How the gravestone is unveiled, like art, on the first anniversary of a death, on the day the soul returns to earth to pay a visit to the living. On this day, we're to pray for the deceased, prayers that will take the soul to God. Prayers like letters of recommendation.

"So why didn't you go?" Henry asks.

"Because I wasn't invited," I say.

Henry takes my hand. "Oh," he says. "I'm sorry," and then he has an idea. "Why don't you hold your own memorial service for your mother? For yourself. At home."

"No." I shake my head. "It wouldn't work out." Dora and Estella never did like my mother. Although she was only a child when they died, Dora has told me more than once that my mother was a loathsome little brat who was stuck on herself, an assessment which is not entirely unimaginable. If I were to light a candle in my mother's memory, Dora would extinguish the flame.

As if it were a matter of taking turns, time at bat, Henry asks if I want to cry now. "Maybe you want to get it out," he says. "It might make you feel better."

Maybe it would make me feel better, but I cannot cry for my

mother. I cannot and I will not cry for my mother. I squeeze Henry's hand. Reassurance. "I'm fine," I tell him. "Really. I am."

On some matters, Henry exhibits the sensitivity of a brick. On this one, however, it would appear he is astute. "If you can't cry for your mother, cry for yourself, Lila. Cry for the love you never got. For the love you never gave. Cry for the love lost."

"Henry," I say, "the only crying that's going to come is from my stomach. I'm starving." I stand up and wipe at my behind as if to brush away debris. "Let's go for dinner." I extend my hand to him, and he takes it, holds on to it, and hand in hand we walk east in search of a place to eat.

14

fabliau: A short story in verse, usually in octosyllabic couplets, relating a comic or bawdy incident from middle-class life.

AFTER DINNER, BACK AT HENRY'S place, in his bed, I urge Henry to think. "You have to have fantasies," I insist. "Everyone has fantasies. It's a well-documented fact."

Yet Henry contends that he does not have fantasies, that he is perfectly content with average sex, whatever that is.

"You're holding out on me," I accuse, and eventually I prod him to take baby steps into the recesses of his libido. "Maybe," he concedes, "I might like it if you dressed up like a nurse."

To each his own, I always say. The nurses who cared for my mother were dedicated women, each with thick ankles and lumpy flesh and they reeked of antiseptics. "A nurse? With a polyester uniform that retains the smell of perspiration?" I ask. "And a cap? And waffle-soled shoes? Like that?"

"Yes. Like that," Henry says. "The white uniform and definitely the cap, but maybe not the waffle shoes. I'd probably like pointy-toed shoes better. With high heels. But maybe not."

I've been trying without much success to teach the games to Henry. The games that involve belts, ropes, bedposts, and radiators, but he resists being led down that path. "What if I like it?" Henry asks, and I say, "That is the idea. To like it."

"No. I mean what if I really like it? Really, really like it?" Henry is worried that I will make him into a pervert and there will be no turning back. What if, after me, he has to resort to paying for a particular sort of pleasure? Suppose he is reduced to answering advertisements from the back pages of *Screw* magazine? Imagine if he were to become a denizen of The Dungeon or The Vault or any one of those dimly lit basement sex clubs featuring slave auctions and free medical exams. "What if," Henry asks, "I discover I can no longer enjoy normal relations?"

"And just what exactly are normal relations?" I want to know.

Henry and Dawn had normal relations. Give or take, depending on Dawn and her mood, they had normal relations twice a week. Two standard-positioned boinks every seven days. Standard positions were those not requiring gymnastic abilities or anything Dawn considered vulgar, such as doggie style. If she were feeling especially generous, Dawn would give his dick a lick. This is what Henry calls normal relations. Go figure. "What about you and Max?" he asks.

"Max—may he rest in peace—and I . . . no, we did not have normal relations. So tell me," I sit up, alert with curiosity. "On the nights when you did not have normal relations, what did you and Dawn do for fun?"

Henry avoids looking at me, and he says, "Different things."

"Such as?" I ask for the specifics. I want the gory details because that is the stuff of life and poetry. The horror of the day-in and the day-out, which I assume can parody itself without any help from me.

"Television," Henry says. "There. Are you happy? We watched television."

"Why would I be happy that you spent your free time watching television with your wife?" I ask. "How does that enrich my life any?"

"We didn't only watch television," Henry informs me. "Some nights we went to the movies or had dinner out. And once a month we got together with three other couples to play Hearts or All-Fours."

"Hearts or All-Fours?" A gleam ignites in my eye. The spark of genuine interest which says ah, now you're talking. "Hearts or All-Fours. How does that go?" I ask.

"Those are card games, Lila. Hearts is a card game and All-Fours is another card game." Henry's tone is one of chastisement. As if I am an ever-so-bad girl for not knowing the names of card games. "The same as poker and bridge are card games," he says. "We got together to play cards. Don't you ever play cards?"

"No," I tell him. "But once I took a quiz in a magazine, and one of the questions was *If you could enter a painting and become a part of it, which painting would it be?*"

"Van Gogh's *Starry Night*," Henry says, even though I hadn't posed the question to him, and I say, "Well, I picked that one with the dogs playing poker."

"But why?" Henry wants to know. "If you don't like card games and you don't want a dog."

"It's the pairing of the two. Because this would be playing poker *with* dogs," I explain. "Plus, it's a high-stakes game and they are drinking heavily. Starry nights are readily available," I tell him. "High-stake card games with dogs are not."

"We played board games too," Henry says. "With dice," he adds as if I might not know from a board game. "Monopoly," he tells me, "and Trivial Pursuit." Henry smiles sheepishly, embarrassed at how ordinary it was; his marriage, his sex life, his fun. Then something occurs to him. "You're not going to write about this, are you?" he asks. "This, my marriage with Dawn, it's not going to show up in a poem, is it?"

I can't swear that it will never show up in a poem because who knows what does, and what does not, make for good material. Often, subject matter will take me by surprise, but I don't mention that. Instead I say, "Write about what? Trivial Pursuit? I hardly think so."

"Yeah, well." Henry leans toward the defensive side, as if I've mocked him and his marriage. Which I suppose I did. "What did you and Max do in the evenings? For fun," Henry challenges me, which could be a mistake on his part. It's as if Henry does not know that there are alternatives to everything under the sun.

"Fun?" I say. "Max and I did not have fun. No. What we had, you could not call it fun."

I did not experience love in the ordinary events of the day. For Max and me, it was not to be found in sharing a movie, a board game, Chinese food delivered, and it's not in Henry's world, the sort of passion that devours you whole. Rather than frustrate himself trying to imagine what it was like for me to be married to Max, he gives that up for a different, but similar, idea. Henry, bless his soul, slides down along the length of the bed and parts my legs.

Max used to go at me like between my legs was his private Wailing Wall. His personal shrine to the six million, and he offered up nibbles and kisses of atonement. If I had to pick one thing I missed most about being married to Max, there you have it.

I lift my head to watch Henry. His nose and mouth are concealed from my line of vision, and his eyes are closed as if lack of sight enhances the remaining senses—touch, taste, tone, smell. Because I don't want to miss out on something, I too close my eyes, and I concentrate. With my nose in the air, I sniff as if I were trying to pick up the scent in the wind, and I cock my ear expecting the sound of Henry's tongue-lapping to be amplified. I ought to be able to hear something similar to the whales' song from down there.

Except I don't hear a thing. It must be a myth, that business about the blind having an acute audial ability. However, after your eyes have been closed for a while, when you open them, you do see things you never saw before. The way I see now, for the first time, that Henry is losing his hair. On the crown of his head, he's got a bald spot. One inch in diameter. I wonder if, without hurting his feelings any, I can suggest to him that he give minoxidil a try when an ooooh escapes from that unnamed part of me. I go gooey into Henry's mouth.

Moving upward along the air-conditioned sheets, Henry plants a kiss on my lips and he makes mention, "You're very well groomed down there."

Henry is such a sweetie-pie. I kiss him on his chest, and between that kiss and the next one, I whisper, "Minoxidil."

Henry sits up fast and without warning. My lips miss their mark, and I'm kissing the air. "What?" Henry asks. "What did you say?"

"Minoxidil," I repeat, but tentatively now. "Have you considered giving minoxidil a try? For that sparse patch. Here." I reach over and tap lightly the spot. "Where you're losing your hair." Henry flinches under my touch, as if the bald spot were sore. "You're balding here." I state the obvious. Then it feels like the right time to add, "You know, I'm in love with you. Really in love. I've never been in love like this before. It's like a miracle," I say, and Henry laps this up as he did my pooch. With elation and enthusiasm. "Really?" he says. "I'm in love with you too."

Never mind that I'm not in love with Henry. I profess to be because I want to be in love with Henry. If I were to be in love with Henry, it would alleviate the void. Perhaps not fill the emptiness, but ease the fear of it. As it is, I worry that I am like one of those women who can't orgasm, that old story of which we've all heard tell. The one of the frigid woman who goes from man to man to man in search of the big O. Practically an infinite number of men and all types. The mailman, the meter reader, the boy who delivers groceries, the husbands of friends and neighbors, and still nothing. At wit's end, she makes an appointment with a sex therapist, who listens to her plight, takes notes, and sends her home with manuals, diagrams, and a bag of toys. Two weeks later she emerges from her bedroom. Her pussy is bruised and battered. She is disheveled and exhausted and more than slightly crazed. Her eyes spin, but no dice. She did not orgasm, but that hardly matters anymore.

Because our best descriptions of the universe are based on theories which incorporate improbability, I profess love for Henry. Given an infinite number of events, the improbable could become a certainty. Which allows me to hold dear the premise that if I continue to toss teacups in the air, eventually one will loop-dee-loop overhead in a dance defying gravity. So if I tell Henry that I love him, and if I repeat that I love him over and over again, it is theoretically possible that one day I will indeed feel such a thing for him.

"But what about your husband?" Henry asks. "Weren't you in love with him?"

I refuse to talk about what I felt for Max because there is no use crying over water under the bridge.

Crying over water under the bridge. That's a Max-ism. The sort of goof he used to make which caused me to melt, but I push the thought away. I don't want Max barging in on an otherwise amiable moment, so I turn my back on him and snuggle up against Henry. "So," I ask, "do you think you'll try it?"

"Try what?"

"The minoxidil," I say. "Because really, you never know what works and what doesn't until you give it a go."

15

···

heptameter: A line of 7 feet, metrically identical to the septenary. The meter exists in classical Greek and Latin prosody. It flourished in the narrative poetry of the Elizabethans. On the whole, however, it has proved unsuitable for the long and elevated verse narrative because of its tendency toward monotony.

"How did it go?" Leon asks about the conference, the one in New Jersey, where I was one of five panelists. Two poets, one editor of a second-rate poetry journal, and two scholars.

I wrinkle my nose. "We spent hours arguing whether the poet first chooses a form in which to write or does the form take its shape from the poem, the content or mood or whatever."

"And what did you conclude?" Leon wants to know.

"We concluded nothing because there is nothing to conclude. The classicists held tight to decorum. Horace's notion of form needing to suit the subject. That you can't write an epic about any old *schmuck*. But really, it's the chicken and the egg all over again," I tell Leon. "Who knows? Who cares? And why ask me? I've written nothing in three years." Then I give Leon the good news. "However, I am madly and passionately in love with Henry. It's been five days now, that I've been in love," I say, and Leon purses his lips in disapproval. "Who do you think you're kidding?" he asks, and I tell him, "No one yet. Except for Henry, of course. He believes me."

"And why did you tell Henry you're in love with him? What was your motivation, might I ask?" Leon tries to act tough, like he's giving me the third degree.

"I was trying it on for size. To see how the shoe fit."

"And how did it fit?"

"Let's put it this way," I tell Leon. "They are comfortable shoes. We're not talking Maud Frizon here. No bows, no kicky heels. Not the sort of shoe I favor. I go for jazzy shoes, but you might like them. They're, well, ordinary. I reject the ordinary. However, I'm hoping I can embellish on them. Add buckles or eventually a dye job. A shade of purple."

Leon says I reject the ordinary because I don't trust it, but what's not to trust? It's slow and steady and oh-so-there. My rejection of the ordinary has zip to do with trust and everything to do with visual clarity. The way I see it, there is little sorrier than couples joining together for the purpose of playing Trivial Pursuit. That is no kind of life. "It's like that old adage," I say, "about how you can't keep them down on the farm after they've been to Paris."

"So being married to Max was like living in Paris?"

"Yeah," I say. "Like when Paris was burning."

So maybe I know nothing of love, of how it's supposed to be. Maybe I did miss out on that lesson. The way you have to read Hermann Hesse when you are seventeen or don't bother. And maybe it is like missing your train, and there you are all alone on the platform, weighted down with your suitcase. Still that doesn't mean you'll gladly hop the next train, because that one might be bound for Normal, Illinois, and you don't want to go there. "I reject the ordinary," I tell Leon, "because the ordinary is tedious and sad."

Leon places his fingertips together to form a diamond. A sure sign that he's about to say something he considers profound. One of those nuggets of wisdom of which he is inordinately proud, the way a cat considers a dead mouse to be worth its weight in gold. "But you are sad," he notes.

"Well of course I am sad. No news there, Leon. However, I notice you didn't say I was tedious."

Leon shifts in his chair. "Explain to me," he says, "what is so tedious about a so-called normal love life?"

I eyeball Leon up and down the way a movie camera pans in on a close-up, taking in his lace collar, his floral-print skirt, his bone-colored pumps, and I say, "I don't know, Leon. You tell me."

Leon chooses to ignore my innuendo, and I can't blame him. It was a rude thing for me to say. Not to mention cruel even, and once said, I regretted it.

"I don't think there's anything awful about being married to a nice guy," Leon says. "Having a nice house, a couple of kids, some good friends to socialize with. What's so awful about two people sharing a life, growing old together with the knowledge that they are loved?"

"Even if I were to concede that there is nothing awful about such a life, which I am not about to concede," I state my case, "you have to admit there's nothing wonderful about it either."

Leon admits no such thing. "I think that it is nice," he says, "to share in the simple pleasures and comforts."

That might be Leon's fantasy, but it's one that gives me a dose of the creeps. "Stop right there, Leon. I can't listen to this anymore. You're breaking my heart."

"Why? Why does this break your heart?" Leon sounds as if he's pleading with me over a really important matter.

"Because," I say. "Because. Because." I need to come up with something. "Because it's so ordinary. It's timid, and when those people get old, they're going to look back and be horrified at their own banality. They'll see that they wasted their lives on the mundane, and they will face death with great remorse. Remorse that they will take to their graves."

"And what," Leon asks, again with the poised fingertips, "will you be taking with you to your grave?"

Carmen jokes about how she is going to take it all with her to the grave. She intends to check out the way the ancient Egyptians did. To arrange for her worldly goods to be buried with her. Like that Japanese businessman who paid record prices for a van Gogh and a Renoir only to announce that when he died, he wanted the paintings to be cremated along with his body.

"A cell phone would be a good thing to take," I tell Leon, and Leon says, "You're making light, Lila."

"Only God can make light, Leon. The rest of us, all we can do is live with it."

Although I don't foresee the need to take my cosmetics or shoes or even my books to the grave, I hardly want to be buried with only regrets.

"Of course you don't," Leon is all empathy here in a way that puts me on my guard. "But you still haven't explained why an ordinary life should engender regret. And why, if the ordinary repels you, are you attempting to love Henry?"

"I'm attempting to love Henry because I like him. He might have hidden potential."

"And?" Leon is waiting for me to tell him the real reason I eschew the ordinary, but I can't do that. I'm embarrassed to admit it lest Leon think I'm an asshole. It's because I want, so desperately want, to be special. Somebody special. I was in *People* magazine. A two-page spread, and it's not like *People* magazine profiles poets every day of the week either. That should count for something, but it doesn't. So like I'm some kind of party doll, I say, "I want to live a life of consequence."

"You want to be loved," Leon notes. Then he says, "When a person is ravenous, he does not dream of a bowl of rice or a loaf of bread. He hungers for a sumptuous meal, a medley of tastes and aromas. A meal for a king."

"Yes," I concur. "Why dream of mere sustenance when you can dream of a feast?"

"Because," Leon says, "the ravenous person is often delusional, and to gorge himself on meats and sweets would make him sick."

I shake my head. I reject what Leon is saying because I have to. "The ordinary life is a trap," I say. "It is to settle for second best. I want to be free to find more than that." I say this with a straight face, but Leon laughs.

"Free? Free? You?" Leon laughs some more, and then he stops laughing. "You're kidding yourself, Lila. You know you're kidding yourself. Free. You're not free to explore so far as the tip of your nose. You're trapped, Lila. You are trapped inside prison walls. Walls of your own construct. Walls that you built brick by brick all by yourself. You live in a fortress surrounded by a moat filled with man-eating beasts. It's no different than when you were married to Max and you made that into a jail cell too. Max didn't lock you in the apartment. *You* locked yourself in. You're a princess shut away in the tower of self-imposed exile. No troll, no wicked stepmother, no witch did this. You did it. You've made it so that no one can get to you, and you sure as shit haven't found your way out."

The moment is dense with the reproach, and then I ask Leon, "Are you done?"

"For now," he says. "We're done for now."

16

---

envelope: The pattern is a special case of repetition. A line or stanza will recur in the same or nearly the same form so as to enclose other material. A line or significant phrase may thus enclose a stanza or a whole poem. The effect is to emphasize the unity of the enclosed portion.

So NOW I'M THE PRINCESS SHUT away in a tower. A cloistered nun alone in a room with bare floors and unicorn tapestries on the walls. Unicorn tapestries like those on the Cloister walls in Fort Tryon Park, which is in Washington Heights and where Max and I took our walks. Until I began to refuse, and then Max walked by himself. In rain and in oppressive heat and bitter cold, he walked there because Max favored a daily constitutional and would not be dissuaded from his routine by inclement weather or the climate of a place.

There are those downtown New Yorkers who crack wise about noses bleeding should they venture above 14th Street, as if there were something fabulous about provincial ways. Not me. I was mobile. I went all over the city, including to the outer boroughs. Obedient to the advertising campaign, I do love New York in that way snobs adore Paris, which, as far as I'm concerned, is a city you can keep. I'll take New York, where, yes, the streets do smell, but by and large, the people don't. I even know the major areas of Staten Island, but 187th Street and where? "You live where?" I'd asked Max to run that by me again.

"One hundred eighty-seventh Street and Cabrini Boulevard," he said.

"Is that in the Bronx? It sounds like a Bronx address," I said, but Max told me, "No. It is not in the Bronx. It is west of the Bronx. It is the northern part of Manhattan. It is not quite the tip of Manhattan. The tip of Manhattan is the area of Inwood. I live in Washington Heights."

Washington Heights. That's where Leon was from originally. I'd wormed the story of Leon's life from him in bits and pieces and shards like from a shattered mirror. How his mother fled the Nazis and found refuge in an apartment in Washington Heights, how she was five months pregnant at the time and how she waited for his father to follow, to join her in the new apartment in the new country and to marry her, how he never did get there for which there could have been a variety of excuses and none of them good news. How she had the baby Leon alone in the bathroom, how she went crazy from worry and grief, and how she eventually learned that Leon's father died at Auschwitz, and how on Saturday afternoons the Irish kids from Inwood swarmed like killer bees into Washington Heights to beat the piss out of the Jew kids, and if they got their hands on a German Jew kid—say your prayers. They knocked you down to the ground for being a Jew, and then for being a German, you got your ribs kicked in. The irony there was lost on the Irish kids from Inwood.

Max may have been born and raised in the German spa town of Baden-Baden, but Max knew New York. Which stands to reason given that he made the map. Max designed his user-friendly maps of New York City for the Rand McNally company. Maps that were reprinted into guidebooks or folded up pocket-sized and sold to tourists. Max was good at his job. A born cartographer if you can imagine such a thing, Max was ever mindful of boundaries and lines of demarcation. That's not to say he wouldn't cross one, but he

knew of the displacement difficulties deriving from the reductions
of one map to another. Differences in the size of the symbols alone
can cause problems practically insurmountable. Still, Max was able
to turn the global earth into a flat surface, which is something only
the gods ought to be able to do. "You will take the A train." Max
gave me directions to get from my apartment to his. "The A train is
an express train," he said. "Therefore, barring any unforeseen difficulties, the trip should not take more than twenty-five minutes."

Twenty-four minutes on the dot, and there I was standing on a
wide avenue, the likes of which we don't have downtown. Downtown, the streets are narrow and hectic with commerce and busy
lives. This avenue was residential in both directions. No skyscrapers
of industry loomed large, and there were no department stores or
supermarkets even. As I walked, I passed only a greengrocer, a bakery, and a shoemaker. These were the commercial properties of a
small town instead of Manhattan. Without the hubbub of big-city
congestion, without traffic jams and the push and shove propelling
them faster, the few pedestrians strolled at a leisurely pace. It was as
if they had nowhere to go but around and around the block.

Max was waiting for me in front of his building. A blond Art
Deco apartment house with etched glass doors. After planting a
long and silky kiss on my mouth, he said, "Come. We will take a
walk." Which wasn't exactly what I had in mind to do. "We will
walk to the park," Max said. "It is beautiful there. You will like it
very much."

I will like it very much. That was so cute of him. On that same
trip to Germany, the one where I learned that Heidelberg had two
uneventful decades between 1933 and 1955, I stayed in a small hotel
in Munich. There, in my room, was a sign posted above the bed. *In
case of fire you will not panic.* Which slayed me. As if I could really
obey an order to not panic while flames licked the walls and devoured the velvet drapes.

Parks are not destinations I go out of my way to get to. Quite the
opposite. While I like a park bench, I prefer the ones bolted into a

small patch of asphalt where the only wildlife is the pigeon. Often I will detour to avoid grass and gathering grounds like Washington Square Park, which is infested with a disproportionate number of mimes. The lawns of Central Park offer me only a shortcut from the West Side to the East. It was not likely that Max's park would impress me any, but he slipped an arm around my waist and nibbled on my earlobe, which led me to conclude that I'd follow him anywhere.

Red and pink and yellow flowers were in full bloom, and because I wasn't wearing my glasses, the gardens seemed impressionistic. A Monet painting of Giverny. When out of focus, many things look nicer than they really are. Still, it is probably wiser in the long run to see clearly.

"So this is Fort Tyrone Park," I said.

"*Tryon,*" Max corrected me. "It is called Fort Tryon Park."

"Try-on." My pronunciation was there, but my timbre was off. Like I was the foreigner.

Old people sat on park benches, and it felt as if this day were a holiday. Only it wasn't a holiday. It was that this neighborhood, what with its mom-and-pop shops, its picturesque park, its etched glass doors, was an anachronism. A throwback to a time when women wore hats and white gloves to go to the market and men wore suits and ties even on weekends. When there was a patina of formality to daily living and no such thing as leisure wear. The other curious component here was that if you listened in on the conversations, these people would be speaking gibberish unless you happened to know German.

If you set aside the beatings they took from the Irish of Inwood, the German Jews—those who had wised up to the mood of National Socialism and could afford to get out while they still had a chance—found a haven in Washington Heights. A place safe from harm and where they could have their strudel too. A place where they could be Jewish and German without anyone telling them that a German Jew was an oxymoron.

When the war was over and Europe was a mess and Germany in

even worse shape, you had any number of Germans looking to escape the rubble, the hunger, and in some cases prosecution. And where else to settle but in Washington Heights, where strudel was already for years baking in the ovens, where they were speaking the language, where dachshunds were the dominant dog. Washington Heights became home to the refugees from before the war and then home to the refugees from after the war. Together again. Old friends and neighbors just like it was prior to the troubles.

Holding hands, Max and I ambled along the meandering pathways that rose and fell like waves, and then we climbed uphill again. "Do you know," Max said, "that we are at the second-highest natural altitude in Manhattan?"

I didn't doubt we were high up there, but Max was mistaken to believe this area was really a part of Manhattan. Never mind what the map said. Fort Tryon Park was not a part of Manhattan or even New York State or anywhere in America. Forget longitude and latitude and oceans and mountain ranges and square miles and bedrock and rivers. Lines on a map are all too easily erased and redrawn. New papers can be issued on a whim along with identity cards, passports, yellow stars. Lock, stock, and barrel, you could scoop up that park, set it down on the outskirts of Frankfurt, and no one would be the wiser.

At the path's end, we came to a field of grass where a quadrangle of stone graced with archways rose up like Oz. Like a castle, it was the setting for a fairy tale. "What is that?" I asked.

"The Cloisters." Max was incredulous. "You do not know the Cloisters? It is built from remnants of five separate cloisters, which accounts for the fact that the sections do not match. Rockefeller paid for it as a gift to the city. Inside is home to a hideous collection of medieval French art. Also, this is where the unicorn tapestries are on display. They are very famous tapestries, although I consider them to be very ugly. They are five hundred years old, and they tell a story of love although some art historians think it is the story of Christ. I say it does not matter. They are too ridiculous to argue over."

I didn't pay close attention to Max's words because I was staring up at the far corner window, the sort of window where, legend might have it, a princess was cloistered away from the world. Cloistered away until her prince arrived on the scene to cut her loose. What she didn't know was that all the while she held the key. Perhaps it was sewn into her brassiere or held tight in her fist, clenched so that she could not open her hand. Just the way Dorothy always had the power to go home, although for the life of me I never could figure out why Dorothy wanted to go back to Kansas where no one paid her any attention when she could have stayed on to be a big cheese in the Emerald City. If I had been Dorothy, I'd have dug in the heels on those ruby slippers and said, "There's no place like Oz." Then again, Dorothy probably grew up to fall in love with a farmer from Wichita where she married and had a family and grew old with no regrets.

17

epinicion: An ode of a number of groups of three stanzas each (strophe, antistrophe, epode) commemorating a victory at one of the four great Greek national games. It was sung either on the victor's arrival at his native town or during a solemn procession to the temple or at the banquet especially held to celebrate his victory.

THERE ARE POEMS BASED WHOLLY in the language, where content is piffle. The substance emanates from the style. It's all in the flourish of the formalism, which was what I was thinking of when I mentioned to Max that we ought to get married. As if to put the finishing touches on natural order, the way you ice sugar rosettes on birthday cakes or dot *i*'s and cross *t*'s, I sought after the ritual. As if it were about ceremony. For me, marriage was a nonempirical concept, and Max was all for it. "Yes," he said. "Let us be bound together by law for all eternity," which wasn't exactly how I would've phrased it.

My parents were thrilled. Down past their socks to their toes they were tickled over the news. Tickled and thrilled and very much relieved because my unmarried state was, for them, a source of shame. As if I were a poor reflection on them. As if they'd spawned a flop of a woman whom no man wanted. As if I were the object of pity no less than if I were disfigured or brain damaged or a drug addict.

Not to mention how, thus far, I'd deprived them of the wedding they'd hoped to make. An orgy of food and music and flowers and waiters in military-style uniforms. The sort of wedding where the guests wonder aloud what this shindig must've cost. For all their emulation of Methodists and Presbyterians, my parents never did get the hang of an understated affair, of slim pickings at the buffet table.

Quicker than you could sneeze, Bella had the telephone directory out and on her lap, thumbing through it for caterers, for reception halls, for florists.

I closed the Yellow Pages on her hand, and I broke the remainder of the news. "We're getting married at City Hall," I said. "No frills. No fuss. No guests other than you and Dad and Carmen."

"What about Max's family?" she asked.

"No. No one from Max's family will be there." Only after we had married did Max tell his family about me. That I existed and that we were married. When he got off the phone with them, he said to me, "My parents wish to welcome you into their home."

"How so?" I asked. "As the lampshade? Or as the bathroom soap?"

If my mother were the genie in the bottle, she would have materialized and said, "Okay. You have three wishes. Let me tell you what they are." My wishes, my desires, my thoughts on the subject were blown off like dandelion dust. "You have to invite your brothers," she told me.

"No." I held my ground. "If I invite my brothers, they'll bring the two stepsisters."

"They are not your stepsisters," my mother said as if I didn't know this. "They are your sisters-in-law, and yes, you have to invite them too. After all, they invited you to their weddings."

At Rob and Goneril's wedding, I got drunk and I vomited on the dance floor. Being that she was first on line, it was the bride who bunny-hopped into the mess, which was yet another thing for which I was never forgiven.

"I know where this is headed." I warned my mother that I was onto her. Wedding guests grow like staphylococci, multiplying logarithmically. "How could I not invite Aunt Mitzie and Uncle Dave and Cousin Howard? And as long as I'm having ten or so people there, what's a few dozen more? And how could we ask all those people to come and witness a ceremony without feeding them afterward? That would be rude. And music is always nice with a meal. It doesn't have to be a dance band. Maybe a string quartet."

"Yes. Exactly." My mother agreed enthusiastically with the sentiments all her own, to which I said, "Exactly not a chance. It isn't going to happen. You can forget about it." When dealing with my mother, you had to cut her off at the knees. Otherwise, she'd walk all over you.

The next step she took was a boycott. It was now possible that she might not be able to attend my wedding. She had a previous engagement scheduled for that day. "Thursday," she said. "I have my ceramics class on Thursdays. We're doing blue glaze. I can't miss blue glaze. Who gets married on a Thursday afternoon anyway? I never heard of such a thing."

"City Hall," I explained, "is not Lenord's of Great Neck. City Hall is not open on weekends."

"No one said anything about Lenord's of Great Neck, so quit being snide. You know perfectly well that I would never make you a wedding at Lenord's of Great Neck."

Lenord's of Great Neck was the place to have a wedding or bar mitzvah if you were long on cash and your tastes ran rococo. A mammoth catering hall done up in gold leaf and crystal chandeliers.

Back when I was in high school, it was *de rigueur* for the suburban princesses to hostess extravagant sweet sixteen parties. Mindy Leffert had her sweet sixteen bash at Lenord's of Great Neck. Which no one could top. Also for her sixteenth birthday, Mindy had her nose done by Dr. Diamond, the nose job king who did Marlo Thomas's nose. A majority of the girls in my school had their noses done by Dr. Diamond. If you looked at the photos in the

yearbook, you'd think there was inbreeding going on in Westchester County. Not only were all these girls sporting the identical
nose, but the surgery lent them a cross-eyed look because Dr. Diamond cut his noses small. I refused to have my nose done despite
my mother's assurance that Dr. Diamond wasn't the only plastic
surgeon in New York. "You can have another nose besides his," she
promised, but I liked my nose as it was. As it has remained. It is a
prominent nose, but I think it is a fine one. My mother wanted me
to have it fixed, she called it fixed as if it were broken, for the same
reason she, in the privacy of her own home, referred to Lenord's of
Great Neck as "kike heaven." In Bella's estimation, my nose was
too too Jewish.

I got up from the country-yellow kitchen table and refilled my
coffee cup. "Look," I said to my mother, "I'd like you to be there
when I get married, but the decision is yours to make."

The same way you take a number at the bakery, you get a number
too at City Hall. A queue for love. Max and I were twenty-third on
the list to be married on that Thursday, and the wait would be over
an hour long. None of us had thought to bring a book to read.

The waiting room decor was in the style of Soviet Realism,
function over form, and the carpet was the color of liverwurst. In a
row we sat like sparrows on a telephone wire. Twittery and poised
for flight at the slightest provocation.

My parents, having capitulated, both wore good navy blue suits.
Max's suit was charcoal gray. His nod to the joy of the day was his
tie. It boasted teal blue bubbles against a burgundy background.
Carmen was overdressed, which is her habit. Carmen favors clothes
with sequins and metallic threads. The bride wore a slinky little
black number.

Surreptitiously and her eyes darting around the room, my
mother snapped open her pocketbook. As if she were going for a
gun from between her Fendi wallet and matching Fendi cosmetic
bag, she retrieved her monkey, which was a weapon of another sort.

Four inches tall, and the way you'd hold an infant or a potted plant, she set it on her lap.

As if doubting his peripheral vision, Max pulled me close and whispered, "What is that which your mother is holding?"

"Meryl," I said. "That's Meryl."

For a toy monkey, Meryl had an impressive wardrobe. Color-coordinated outfits with matching accessories. In an unprecedented burst of maternal flair Bella had rescued Meryl from a pile of cast-off toys at a yard sale. Lavished with mother-love and attention, Meryl slept in a basket on my mother's night table. Its kumquat-sized head rested on a powder-puff pillow, and a square of red cashmere cut from an old scarf served as a blanket. When Meryl was not asleep in the basket, it was with my mother. In her purse or on her lap or sitting next to her in the passenger's seat of Bella's BMW.

"Oh, I love her gown." Carmen fingered the satin of the monkey's dress. "Is it new?"

For the occasion of my marriage to Max, Meryl was dolled up in a frilly purple frock with a matching straw hat. Dangling from its wrist was a lavender plastic handbag which looked suspiciously like the handbag belonging to the Barbie of my childhood. As if my mother had stolen my Barbie's purse to give to Meryl. Which was something I wouldn't have put past her.

Smoothing out the folds in Meryl's party dress, my mother leaned forward to catch my eye. To gloat. Luxuriating in her triumph, her message was both implicit and twofold. Not only had she managed to sneak in a guest without my permission, but get a load of the affection of which my mother was capable. How she might have loved me too had I only been the sort of daughter that Meryl was—had I been well behaved, had I worn nice outfits with matching accessories, and had I had a nose so itty-bitty as to barely be a nose at all.

18

----

four ages of poetry: An essay by Thomas L. Peacock in which he declares that classical Greek and Latin verse passed through the ages of (1) iron, or crude primal vigor, (2) gold, or Homeric mastery, (3) silver, or Virgilian refinement, and (4) brass, or "the second childhood of poetry."

I'M FLIPPING THROUGH THE PAGES of *Vogue* magazine on the lookout for a hairstyle that catches my attention. Something for the season which is proving to be humid as well as hot. Dora has been after me to bob my hair, but she's very much a product of her day. She considers a bob to be the bee's knees, but I'm thinking along the lines of a kicky flip. If I ever do cut my hair, that is. It's been years since I've had so much as a trim. Not since Max and the Bergen-Belsen crop. Meanwhile, Kevin combs my hair free of tangles. A pink plastic cape is tied around my neck and covers me like a tarp. Kevin is the man who colors my hair Black Cherry. Black Cherry to break up the monochrome of my naturally black hair, only now Kevin has an announcement to make. "Gray. You're going gray, Lila. Look at this. Three of them here." Kevin isolates silver hairs from the crown of my head for me to witness. I shut my eyes against the onslaught, and I beg of him, "Do something."

"Don't you worry." Kevin pats my shoulder to reassure me. "I'll make it like they were never there." A promise which he keeps. I examine the roots. Kevin is a genius with color and I tell him that.

"Lila," he says, "it wasn't much. Only a few hairs." Such modesty, and I double his tip before dashing out the door because I was expected at Henry's twenty minutes ago.

"Sorry I'm late," I say. "I got hung up with some things."

"No problem." Henry is smiling like he's got a secret concealed behind his back. Which he does. It is his daughter hiding behind his legs. The girl peeks out and giggles at me before retreating back to where she considers herself eclipsed from my view. His son comes and stands at his side. Both children are wearing flannel pajamas, the sort with the feet attached. "Isn't it a bit on the warm side for those pajamas?" I ask. The children ought to be naked because the night air is thick and sultry. My hair sticks in ringlets to the nape of my neck.

"They've got the air conditioner going full blast in their room," Henry tells me. "It's like the Arctic Circle in there."

I don't like air-conditioned rooms. Summer ought to be hot. Not to mention the way bacteria spreads through the air conditioner's filtering system. Also, I am not keen on this introduction to Henry's children, for which I was not prepared. Thus far, I'd managed to avoid them, but for weeks now Henry has been after me to make their acquaintance. Having run dry of excuses, all that remained was the truth, which wasn't going to wash. There was no polite way to tell him that I don't mix with children and I don't make exceptions to my own generalizations. Parents, I have learned, are offended by that kind of candor.

It's not that I actively dislike children. It's that I don't go stupid for them. Still, parents tend to consider my position to be that of a witch. Like I must be plotting to boil the kiddies in a stew pot along with carrots and parsnips. That I'm all for thin gruel as sustenance for orphans, and each day at sunrise I hook up a toddler to a plow designed for oxen.

Rather, I feel about children as I do about dogs. They deserve to have a warm bed in which to sleep. They have an inalienable right to be fed tasty and nutritious meals. I want for each of them to have a chew toy of their own, and it's best for all concerned if they attend obedience school. Children and dogs deserve to be loved, but not by me. I am not interested in having them slobbering and sniffing at my crotch. This is not to say I don't enjoy being slobbered over or having my crotch sniffed. It's a different order of business when men do those things. For starters, when a man drools over me, it's not usually a literal event. Children and dogs, on the other hand, they leave a puddle.

Max and I talked of having children on only one occasion. Not seriously talked of it, but hypothetically the way lovers sometimes pick features for a baby as if off a Chinese menu. Your eyes, my nose, my hair, your hands. There, we stopped because our marriage did not allow for the intrusion of another person, not even one of our making or of our imaginations.

"Lila"—Henry makes introductions all around—"this is Pollack." He places his hand on the boy's head, and then reaches around his back and slides his daughter into view. "And this," he says, "is Cosima."

Pollack and Cosima. Such conceit, these names. Refusing to yield to the pretensions, I nod in greeting and I say, "Hello, Polyp. Hello, Eczema," which they seem to find amusing, although Henry does not. "You shouldn't make fun of them," he tells me, and I tell him, "I'm not making fun of them. I'm making fun of you."

At least with dogs, you don't have to make conversation. The main difficulty I have with children is that once we get beyond the initial greeting, I never know what to say to them. Frankly, I don't give a rat's ass what grade they are in at school or if they like their teachers or not. I doubt we have shared interests, and who wants to be the recipient of an observation regarding your size? I am not entirely insensitive. I would never say, "My, my. You are such a big girl," because no one wants to hear that.

For reasons of their own which are well past my grasp, Polyp and Eczema are all over me like something sticky. Henry is beaming like Telstar transmitting an episode of family happiness. The children want to play with me, and they want to show me their toys. Eczema has a game called "Pretty, Pretty Princess," of which she is most enamored. "I used to be a princess," I tell her. "A real princess."

Her eyes go wide as the sea, and I say, "Hold your water, kid. I'm not a princess anymore. I used to be one, but I abdicated."

Polyp wants to know the definition of abdicated, and I tell him, "It means that I quit. Not everyone is cut out for the princess way of life."

Henry snorts because he cherishes the notion that my abdication is in name only. That I gave up the title but maintain the holdings. Then, Henry disappears into the kitchen, and alone with the children, I open my purse. Like a magician producing a pair of doves from up a sleeve, I pull out a chocolate bar. Which was going to be my dinner, but I snap it in half. The way a toad's tongue flicks long and fast to snatch a bug mid-flight, two sets of greedy and grubby little hands grab hold of the chocolate. "Can we eat this now?" Eczema asks me.

Polyp aims to be mature and well behaved. "Daddy doesn't let us have candy after dinner," he says.

"Well," I tell them. "I'm overriding Henry's veto on this one. I say it's okay to eat the candy now. Go ahead." I egg them on. What do I care if their teeth rot?

When the chocolate is nearly devoured, when each of them has but one bite left plus their fingers to lick, I go back to my purse for two five-dollar bills. "This is the deal," I lay it out. "There's a five spot in it for each of you to stay in your room and go to sleep."

"But I'm not tired," Eczema says, and I say, "Then pretend you are asleep. If you don't," I warn, "then I'll take back the money and I'll rat you out about the chocolate."

In this respect, children are like wartime whores. There are no depths they won't sink to in exchange for a couple of bucks and a

Hershey bar. Also they want to steer clear of the authorities.

Henry comes into the living room with a glass of wine in each hand. He places the goblets on the coffee table. Henry uses coasters. "Where are the kids?" he asks.

"Sleeping," I say, and we both grin at the good fortune of that. We sit on the couch. Henry sips his wine and says, "They like you. I can tell."

"That's nice." I take a sip of wine too. Henry has a gift for picking a good wine from the sale rack.

"So." Henry leans back into the cushions. "Tell me. How was your day?" Henry has what he considers to be good manners. He thinks it is only polite to inquire about my day, that it would be boorish of him to skip such niceties in favor of lunging at me. As if I would find him rude were he to push me to the floor, one hand racing up my skirt, without first having asked after my day. Max, too, always asked about my day, but later. For Max, the inquiry was postcoital. The way having a cigarette is something you do after sex. Not before.

"Fine," I tell him. "My day was fine," and he wants to know, "Aren't you going to ask about my day?"

"No," I say. "I'm not going to ask about your day. At least not now."

Finally, Henry comes in for a kiss. His hand cups my breast, which causes me to groan. "Shhh," Henry whispers. "You'll wake the kids."

It's come to this for me. I have reached the stage in life, that age where I'm expected to keep my yearnings quiet lest I wake the kids, and in his wallet the man in my life carries pictures of his children in lieu of condoms.

I slip from the couch to the carpet and I'm on my knees. I unzip Henry's fly, and after a few teasing flicks of my tongue, I take the whole of him in my mouth. I'm having a fine time here when out of nowhere my jaw pops, and an excruciating pain shoots between my mandibular fossa and the temporal bone, the dislocation of the temporomandibular joint, and I see stars. "Shhh," Henry says again, and for the second time in ten minutes I am told to hush my body's responses to physical stimulation because his children are in the next room feigning sleep.

As the pain subsides, the misery index rises as if pain and misery were two sisters on the seesaw. The kind of misery that comes from the realization that I am aging, growing older, a point from which there is no return. I blame time for the sore spot and for interrupting this blow job. I am distressed at how I'm going from youth to middle age. "Just like that," I snap my fingers. "That fast, it's happening." Overnight, and it is as distressing as it would be to discover that, no longer having control of your functions, you are wearing adult diapers. "My next birthday, I'll be thirty-five. Thirty-five," I mock-shout. "That's halfway to seventy. I'm on the precipice, Henry," and Henry asks, "When is your birthday?"

I tell him the date of my birthday, and Henry suggests that a jaw can pop at any age, even when you're very young. "I think you're making a mountain out of a molehill, Lila."

"*Mogul.* Mountain out of a mogul," I say softly, and mostly to myself.

"What did you say?" Henry asks, and I tell him, "It has to be age-related because it has never happened before. Then I blurt out, "I'm going gray. My hair. It's going gray."

Henry comes in for a closer look. "No you're not," he says. "You haven't any gray hair at all."

Because no way do I want him to know about Kevin, which is my personal business, I say, "I am too getting old," and I sulk and pout, and as if it's Henry's fault, I add, "and I never have any fun anymore."

"Gee. Thanks," Henry says. On the snide side, and he covers himself with a pillow.

"Not you. Not this. I mean the other kinds of fun. Things we did when we were younger. I want to feel young again."

"Yeah," Henry concurs. "To not have a worry in the world.

Such innocence. Little angels, and all they do is play. Like my kids."

"No," I say. "Not that young." I have no interest in being a child, and I wonder what worries in the world could Henry possibly have. "I want to have the sort of fun that was a really great time back then," I tell him, "but it wouldn't be any fun now."

I mean fun like hitchhiking through Europe and sleeping in youth hostels, which never have private bathrooms. Fun like hanging out in Washington Square Park as if it were cool to be mentally deficient. Fun like dyeing my hair neon blue. Fun like fucking eleven different boys in a one-week stretch, and fun like drinking cheap red wine until I puke on my shoes. That kind of fun.

Not to mention all the fun stuff I never did get around to doing, and now it's too late. Already I'm past the expiration date to be a ballerina or a rock star or a topless dancer.

It's as if I'm watching time fly by the way Salvador Dalí painted a clock with wings. I want to reach out and grab it. I want to keep it still to my breast as if I could hold the meter of time the way I can hold my breath. Henry rests his hand on my shoulder. "Are you okay?" he asks. "You look as if you're about to cry."

"I want to do something fun," I tell Henry, and to my surprise, he has a plan. He offers us a chance to recover things lost. My youth, and his mother's jewelry. "My mother wasn't dead for an hour before my Aunt Adele came over and took it all. She said that it was her jewelry and that my mother had borrowed it, which was not true. My mother wouldn't have borrowed a cup of sugar from her sister. Adele stole that jewelry, and I was too distraught at the time to do anything about it."

While some people might meet such a story with skepticism, I know from firsthand experience that death invites a thief.

Once a month Henry and his children have lunch with Aunt Adele. For Henry, it is fulfilling a familial obligation. For his children, it is torture. He suggests that I join them the next time, which happens to be tomorrow. Together we can ransom his mother's jewels.

"Now?" I ask. "Suddenly you want to embark on a crime spree?"

After a pause for the full dramatic effect, Henry tells me, "It wouldn't be the first time. When I was a kid, twelve and thirteen, my friend Marsh and I broke into apartments. Neighbors' apartments. Breaking and entering. We'd wait to see who went out, and then we'd go in. Through a window."

Perhaps there is common ground for Henry and me after all. When I was twelve and thirteen, I was an accomplished shoplifter who could've gone professional. Reflex-active and like my fingers were made of sticky tape. From Lord & Taylor and Bonwit Teller and from Woolworth, I clipped cosmetics, costume jewelry, scarves, and trinkets. Strictly for the thrill of it because I wanted for nothing, and most of my booty was crap that wound up in the garbage as soon as I got it home. "What did you steal?" I ask Henry. "Money? Television sets? Priceless antiques?"

"Nothing. We never took anything." Henry says they were after only the kick of entering and rifling through personal effects. Fingering bras and panties. Sometimes they got lucky and turned up a copy of *Penthouse*, going lightheaded over the beaver shots.

Max stole something once. An avocado. From a Korean fruit market, and he got nabbed. "I have no idea why I did such a thing," he said. "I never understood what was the impulse which possessed me, but I chose an avocado and then on my way to the cash register, I put it in my jacket pocket instead of paying for it. It was not even a good avocado. It was bruised on the skin so the flesh would have brown spots. It was very humiliating when the man stopped me at the door and pulled the avocado from my pocket. It was lucky for me that he did not call the police."

When I was finished laughing I told Max, "This is New York, Max. No one is going to call the police over the theft of a piece of fruit."

Decidedly excited at the prospect of risk, I say to Henry, "Count me in," and I wonder if maybe I could love Henry for real.

19

catalogue verse: A term used to describe lists of persons, places, things, or ideas which have a common denominator such as heroism, beauty, death with artistic intention, such as indicating the vastness of a war. It has been used for the sake of whimsy or because the poet enjoyed the sound of particular kinds of words, e.g., the list of jewels in Wolfram von Eschenbach's *Parzifal*.

THE DOORMAN ANNOUNCES OUR arrival with a flourish that matches the gold braids on his uniform, and my high heels make a clickety-click on the marble floor. Behind us, the children take listless steps, as if by moving slowly they might never get there.

Adele gives Henry one of those near-kisses and a hug without actually pressing flesh against flesh. "Henry," she says. "I didn't know you were bringing a friend. What a pleasant surprise," she remarks in a manner which is really a reprimand to Henry. She shakes my hand with a limp three fingers, and she smells of pressed powder and lavender. "Lila," I introduce myself. "Lila Moscowitz."

"Lila is a famous poet," Henry says. "Perhaps you've heard of her?"

Adele takes a moment and poses her index finger to her temple as if she's thinking about that. "No," she says. "I don't place that name. Definitely not." Then she turns her attention to Polyp and Eczema. She reminds them not to touch anything.

Adele has even more stuff than Henry has by a landslide. This could be a gift shop here, the sort that specializes in cut-crystal animal figures and limited-edition plates. The walls are floor-to-ceiling shelves teeming with precious *tchotchkes*. On tabletops, knickknacks are pressed elbow to elbow. The Hummels barely have room to breathe.

Claiming he needs to wash up, Henry leaves me alone with his children and his aunt. Polyp asks if they can watch television, and Adele says, "Yes. You may watch television, but no feet on the couch." They beeline for the TV, and Adele turns to me to say, "They're so ill-mannered, but I suppose all children are these days." Adele's got one of those turkey wattles beneath her chin, and she is wearing a wig that is slightly askew.

"You certainly have some lovely things here," I say. "How do you manage to keep them free of dust?"

"I have a girl," Adele tells me. "A colored girl, you know. She comes to me twice a week. You can't have live-in help anymore. Not these days," she says as if we agree on the dangers of live-in maids and the horrors of modern times.

As if to fill in the empty space made by the lull in the conversation, Adele lifts, from the nearest shelf, a six-inch tree carved from jade. Leaves made from seed pearls hang by gold wire. "We got this in China," she says as though I had asked. "My late husband and I traveled all over the world."

"Really," I say. "My late husband and I, we never went anywhere."

Adele is not about to let my misfortunes get in the way of her recitation. "Oh yes," she says. "Everywhere you can think of, we were there. Everywhere except to Russia."

When Adele says *Russia* I don't think she is referring to the Russia we know today. I think she means the former Soviet Union. This is one of those cases where, if you stay perfectly still, events catch up to you. "My late husband," she tells me, "refused to go to Russia because he would not give those people our money."

"Those people?" I ask.

"The Communists. The Communist people," she tells me as if I were the moron here.

"But you went to China," I make mention. "The Chinese are Communists," and Adele's face is a blank, as devoid of expression as a white dinner plate. Either she did not know that the Chinese are Communists or else she did not know that they are people. Whichever. She excuses herself to check on the soufflé and to add another place setting at the table. "I didn't know Henry was bringing a guest," she says, driving her point home.

Having cased the bedroom, Henry returns to my side. "I couldn't find any of it." He speaks in a stage whisper. "It's a mountain of junk in there."

I cluck over how inept Henry is at the business of thievery, and I tell him, "Leave it to me. I'll do it. After lunch."

The dining room table is set as if for a state dinner. Each place setting has three forks, two spoons, two knives, butter plates, a wine goblet, and a water glass. The soufflé is cheese. Melted globs of cheese displaying the full spectrum of the color orange. The side dish is cinnamon buns coated with sugar icing. To look at them makes my teeth hurt. The children groan at being called away from the television. Maybe something went wrong in the kitchen. Or maybe this is it, what she meant to serve, because she makes no apologies for the splat of cheese she dishes onto my plate.

It must be the way I recoil from the table, as though she's serving up cow droppings, that prompts Adele to ask, "Are you people allowed to eat cheese? If I had known you were coming I would've made inquiry in advance. With advance warning, I would've asked." Adele is proud of her skills as a hostess and of her worldly ways, how she knows fun facts about foreigners. "I know you people have rules about food."

"Oh, we can eat cheese," I tell her. "Except on Saturdays. We can't have cheese on Saturday."

"I'm not eating this ever," Polyp says, and he covers the plate with his napkin.

"Me too." Eczema follows her brother's lead, and Adele points out, "But today is Saturday."

"Oh my. So it is," I say. "Well never mind me. The rest of you enjoy your lunch." The children are content to lick the icing off the cinnamon buns, and I excuse myself from the table. "I need to use the bathroom," I say. The napkin on my lap falls to the floor.

Like Doric columns, four wig stands herald the vanity table in Adele's bedroom. Three of them are topped off with a festival of spit curls. Ash brown spit curls, and the fourth stand is bald. As is, I assume, Adele. My mother wore a wig too. After the chemotherapy, Bella's hair fell out in clumps. "I look like a plucked chicken," she'd told me, and she wept copiously at the loss.

Jars of goop cover the table's surface. Cold creams. Wrinkle creams. Eye creams. Hand softeners. And a big vat of that glop that fades liver spots.

Adele shares her canopy bed with ruffles of white organdy, a ménage of needlepoint pillows, and three dolls. Dolls made for collectors and not for children. Madame Alexander dolls, which spook me. Like poltergeists or demon seeds, they look dead.

I open one of Adele's closets, and I am assaulted by an overflow of outfits in pinks and apricot. From the top dresser drawer spill frillies. Nightgowns and bedjackets in the same baby-pastel color scheme as her clothes. Adele and her bedroom are a tribute to fluff and desperation.

I've lost the enthusiasm for finding the stolen jewelry. Instead, I'm looking just to see what else is here. As if in one of these drawers is a poem for me. An elegy would be the obvious choice, but I'm liking the idea of an ode. A Pindaric ode with the wigs as the chorus, and I open the third dresser drawer.

This could be the loot from a Spanish galleon or the vault at Auschwitz. A treasure chest of jewels. Ropes of pearls and strands of gold are tangled up in knots. Tarnished bracelets encrusted with rubies and sapphires. A ring missing two baguettes on either side of an emerald the size of my eyeball. Diamond earrings separated from their mates. Loose stones galore. I pick up a cameo brooch. A cameo like the one Anna Mason wears. A turn-of-the-century cameo. The shell is cracked.

No one loves Adele. Henry, her only living relative, doesn't even like her. Not so much as a little bit, and the woman hoards gold and gems as if that means she has something valuable. I close the drawer and return to the table.

Adele gets up to make coffee. Eczema is kicking the chair leg, and Polyp wants to know if we can leave now.

"Soon," Henry promises him, and I tell Henry, "It's not there." I slip my hand into my pocket and finger the cameo's fault. "She must have a safety deposit box at a bank," I say. Henry will have to wait until Adele dies to recover his mother's jewelry, and I, having taken only the broken cameo, did not recover anything of my lost youth. Like Max with the avocado, I chose something damaged and of little worth to anyone.

20

epic question: In ancient epic poetry after the theme of the poem is announced, the muse, as patron goddess of the poet, is sometimes asked what started the action. The answer then offers a convenient way for the poet to begin his narration.

LEON IS WEARING A DOVE GRAY dress with gold buttons down the front, nylon hose, and black patent leather flats. As if he works a corporate job. Vice-president of a bank or better yet an assistant district attorney because also he is at ease with the questions. "I'm not clear on this. Did you or did you not have a sweet sixteen party?"

"Not," I say, and Leon notes, "When it's a regular birthday, you want to pull out all the stops, but for the milestones—your sweet sixteen and your wedding—you shy away from celebration. Why do you think that is?"

"I did not shy away from the celebration of my sixteenth birthday exactly," I tell him.

My sweet sixteen bash was set up and ready to roll. The place—Ling Tung's Cantonese Restaurant, which was shaped like a pagoda—the date—Saturday, September 26th—the time, the menu—a smorgasbord of miniature egg rolls, baby ribs, dumplings, and bite-sized egg foo yungs—had been chosen with care and calculation. The invitations were at the print shop when Mindy Leffert's

invitations arrived, hand-calligraphied no less, requesting the pleasure of seventy-six of her dearest friends to join her for dinner and
dancing at Lenord's of Great Neck on Saturday, September 26th.
Who could compete with that? Not me and my greasy miniature egg
rolls. So I called off my party, and I spent my sixteenth birthday in a
prone position, facedown on my bed, weeping and beating my pillow
with my fists.

"You always cry on your birthday," Leon says, but I cannot dis-
cern if he's telling me this or asking me if it's so.

"Not every year. Not the last two, but it's definitely a tradition,"
I say. "Starting with the very first one, I cried."

"You don't remember your first birthday." Leon is incredulous.

I beg to differ. "Oh, I remember it distinctly. Not the day, but
the photographs." That's how it is with memory. We remember not
the events themselves but the pictures of the events and the subsequent retellings. Consequently, all memory is indelible but also
distorted through the lens of the camera or the way the game of
Telephone is played.

In particular, one photograph of me on my first birthday looms
large. By first birthday, I do not mean the day of my birth. Rather, I
mean the day I turned one year old not counting womb time. There
were no pictures taken on the event of my birth, which is a pity. I'd
give my thumbs for that kind of documentation. Or better yet, the
way it's done now, a videotape of the entire episode. Oh, to have
seen the rude awakening, and did I know from the get-go that a
dreadful mistake had been made? The accident of birth. The fickle
wheel of fortune. So easily, I could've been someone else. I could've
been Caroline Kennedy or Princess Stephanie or Anne Frank. As it
stands, I'll never know if I entered the world in a state of confusion
or a fit of conniption. Did the resentment show itself on my newborn expression or did I come into being as an innocent lamb ignorant of the cosmic error perpetrated? "It would be something, to be
able to see that. My birth," I say to Leon, longingly.

Because he asks it of me, I create a narrative from the fragments of memory of the photograph of my first birthday.

It was yellowed, the picture I remember best. Not from age necessarily, but because the quality of the print was poor, and the fine detail had blurred. The essence, however, remained. A conical-shaped pointy paper hat sat on my head. Like a dunce cap. A hat for idiots. A party hat that shared qualities with one of Annette Funicello's breasts. The elastic holding it secure and upright nipped at the baby-soft flesh under my chin. A cake was set out before me. One lit candle dotting the center. They had me dressed in a pink frilly frock which clashed with the ripe rage-red of my complexion. I was bellowing for all get-out. Ear and head-splitting shrieks that penetrated the skin and the soul, forcing me to gulp for air.

"Why do you think you were so sad?" Leon asks. "Do you have any idea?"

"Sad?" I scoff at the thought. "I wasn't sad, Leon. The tears I cried that day were like dry ice. Cold and giving off steam like breath in frigid weather. It was fury. Not sorrow."

Leon tucks his hair behind his ears and reveals a small gold ball on each lobe. "Well then," he asks, "why were you so angry?" and I note, "Leon. You got your ears pierced? You didn't tell me."

"Yes," Leon rolls his eyes toward the heavens as if passing comment about me to God. "I got my ears pierced. Now quit dodging the question. Why do you think," he asks again, "you were so angry?"

I give him a shrug that is genuine. I honestly don't know the answer to his question, and I share the only clue I have. "I once asked my mother about it," I say, "and she told me it was about nothing, that I just wanted attention."

One thing about me which Bella was fond of repeating was how I was a good baby. "Lila," she would say, "was such a good baby. Not like the boys. I would put her in her crib, and I could leave her alone all day and not a peep out of her." My mother swore that until I was nine months old, I never cried. Not once. Not for any reason. Perhaps that was my first mistake. I should have cried then. In the beginning.

"Wanting attention isn't nothing," Leon says, to which I say, "No shit, Leon." Then I add, "They look good. Your ears pierced. It makes for a nice touch."

"Thank you." Leon smiles, but also he is onto me. Not about to let me get away with the backdoor switch, Leon says, "The photograph, Lila. We were talking about the photograph." Then Leon glances at the clock. My time is up, which is a phrase I'm liking less and less lately. "Why don't you bring it with you next week. I'd like to see it for myself."

"And I would be happy to oblige you, but no can do, Leon. It's lost," I tell him. "Forever. To the landfill."

After my mother died and my father bought himself the condominium in Florida, Goneril and Regan spared him the sorry task of sorting through the family treasures. They had experience with that sort of thing, pocketing the wheat and discarding the chaff. Whatever did not have monetary value or obvious necessity of a practical nature got tossed in the trash. Which was their loss. Had they made me an offer, I would've paid them handsomely for that photograph, the proof positive of needs unfulfilled and love unattended.

21

pantoum: A poem of indeterminable length, composed of quatrains in which the second and fourth lines of each stanza serve as the first and third lines of the next, the process continuing through the last stanza. In this quatrain, the first line of the poem also reappears as the last.

SEATED AT MY DESK I GO through the mail, which is something of a high point in my day because you never know what you'll get. A prize, an award, a grant, a miracle, although this batch falls short. I've got here the Con Ed bill, the telephone bill, and a request for a poem from an upstart literary magazine that calls itself *Smashing Sonnets*, which would not have been an entirely stupid name if *smashing* were an adjective. As an adjective, it would've been merely anglophilic. As in, "Oh darling, you've written a smashing sonnet. Simply divine." Alas, the editors make it clear that their *smashing* is a verb. Their letter outlines their mission to "obliterate all tradition in writing including rendering definitions obsolete," which renders them sitting ducks for ridicule. I can't be bothered with this. I haven't the stamina to educate the young, to explain that the obsoletism of definition renders their letter gobbledygook.

Next I open a letter from my friend Sarah, who is spectacularly miserable since having been lured to a state university in Nebraska with the promise of tenure as bait. Also, the day's mail brings me a summons to sit jury duty from the Supreme Court of the State of New York. You have to admire them for their tenacity.

But I can't sit jury duty now. With barely a month of summer to go, this is no time to lose two weeks sitting jury duty. I drop the summons into the wastebasket.

Like every other denizen of New York City, I have blown off the call to sit jury duty on umpteen occasions at least. As a group, we New Yorkers are not keen on the prospect of surrendering two weeks of our lives for the privilege of participating in the system, for which we receive twelve dollars a day. Generally speaking, when the summons arrives we treat it as if it were a circular from Kmart as opposed to an official document from the cornerstone of American justice. Often this is fodder for cocktail party chitchat, the accounts of jury duty being blown off in record numbers.

Mostly I fail to appear when called because I have other things more pressing to do. Like now, I can't go because I might have to start teaching in a few weeks. Suppose I have to prepare course outlines and syllabi and whatnot? They can't rightly expect me to cut the remainder of my vacation short. Another time I was called conflicted with a previous appointment to get my hair colored and you just don't cancel on Kevin. It isn't done. I've been summoned to sit jury duty when I had poetry conferences out of state, and also when I was living in Washington Heights and therefore it wasn't possible to go anywhere.

There were two calls to jury duty when I did have every intention of showing up, but as often is the case, good intentions get thwarted. The first time was when I met Max, and fate had something else in store for me, and then there was that one other time after that when I was prepared to fulfill my civic responsibilities. I'd set my alarm clock, and I went to my closet to choose an outfit, to spare myself from having to pick one out first thing in the morning when I'm not alert and could wind up donning a fashion *faux pas*. Dora came to my side and selected a red velvet cocktail dress. Dora adores velvet, satin, and lace, and again I had to explain to her that women don't dress up like they used to, which makes Dora sad, and me too. Next, Dora followed me to my bookshelves. I needed to pick a book to take with me. Estella got up from the couch to put in her two cents' worth. The few people I knew who actually had sat jury duty issued the identical warning. Bring a book, I was cautioned. Reading material is mandatory because you sit around doing nothing for hours at a clump.

Estella chose *The Portable Dorothy Parker*, which she dropped at my feet. I'd asked her repeatedly not to toss my books around as if they were quips. I picked it up, and flipped through it. Estella has always been a great champion of Dorothy Parker. When she read my poetry, Estella said it wasn't half bad but that I was no Mrs. Parker, that's for sure. I put the book back on the shelf, and Estella vanished in a huff.

When I was first getting recognition as a poet, I was invited to give a reading at the College of Mount Saint Vincent, which is in Riverdale. The fancy part of the Bronx. Already experience had taught me that when reading to college students, do the smut poems. College students go for suck-and-fuck literature. As if exposure to sex in an art form renders them bohemian and mature all in one stroke of self-gratification.

The bus routed for the Riverdale section of the Bronx got caught in a snarl of traffic, the fault of an Audi which died in the left lane. Repeatedly checking my watch, I snorted and jiggled in the seat as if that would get the bus moving.

Sprinting from the college gate to the auditorium, my breasts bobbled under my black sweater, and also set into motion were my earrings, miniature fruit baskets filled with tiny glass bananas, cherries, and oranges, and they continued to swing as I pushed through the door. Nearly every seat in the house was taken up with a body, and I faced the backs of their heads. Not regular heads, but the heads of nuns cloaked in navy blue and white wimples, and I skidded to an abrupt halt. Like you see on the Saturday morning cartoons. Smoke ought to have come from my heels. Mount Saint Vincent was a

Catholic college. I knew that. Saint Vincent and all that goes with it, but I forgot. I forgot about the nuns, and even more than they terrified little Catholic girls, nuns scared the crap out of little Jewish girls in a way that the intervening years had done little to alleviate.

Such a situation offered me two choices. To turn and run back the way I came like film on rewind, or to read smutty poetry to a room dominated by nuns.

I read the smut to the nuns, and afterward at the reception-to-follow where I tried to hide behind a pillar, a short and round one made her way over to me. A silver cross, adorned with Jesus crucified, hung around her neck. I half expected her to hold it out to repel the evil that was me, the way it's done in movies to ward off vampires. The other half of me braced myself for a rap on the knuckles with a wooden yardstick. Instead, she smiled. Not beatifically, as you might think, but impishly as if she were bucking, not to be a saint, but one of Santa's elves. "You were so very wonderful," she said. Her eyes reflected the pleasure of mischief.

Such was my relief that I would've kissed the hem of her gown had she been wearing one, but this nun had opted out of the habit in favor of the sort of outfit Leon wears. A prim white blouse and a gray skirt which fell just below her knee. Not a good area on a nun for me to be kissing in public.

"You see," she said to me, "when it comes to sin, I let Dante be my guide. My Virgil, so to speak. Dante understood sin. Sins of the flesh are minor. Piddling. Barely sins at all. More like transgressions. But take hypocrisy." She wagged the finger of reprimand at the mere mention of the word. "Hypocrisy, now that is evil. And by the way, I love your earrings."

A gush of affection welled up inside me for this nun. This nun who went for smutty poetry and gaudy jewelry. This nun who wanted to roast hypocrites like chestnuts on an open fire, and it was with her in mind that I took *The Inferno* from my bookshelf. It was the right book to bring along to jury duty, to read while I waited to sit in judgment of another man's alleged sins.

Having surfaced from the subway into the harsh glare of the morning, I stood at the corner of Chambers Street and West Broadway to get my bearings. I looked left and then right and then I heard a voice. A very familiar voice, as if it were a disembodied echo. "Follow West Broadway north," the voice said, and before my goosebumps got the chance to rise, I whirled around. That wasn't a voice in the wind. It was Max. My Max. In the flesh.

"Max," I said. "This is so funny. Such a coincidence, you won't believe it. Guess where I'm going? To sit jury duty. What an amazing coincidence."

"Yes," Max said. "This is a coincidence indeed."

As a foreign national, Max was exempt from jury duty and long ago he'd finished with the lower Manhattan project. Already his maps of downtown were gracing the racks on tourist information booths throughout New York City, and so I asked, "What brings you here?"

"You," he said. "You brought me here. I have something for you." Resting his briefcase on top of a garbage barrel as if it were the lid to a pot, he popped the lock. "You'll need to sign these."

Divorce papers. No-fault divorce papers, which was decent of him, in a way. No-fault, considering how he could've placed heaps of fault at my feet. That he could've gotten me on abandonment, at the very least. Not to mention emotional cruelty and breach of promise. Instead, Max was gallant about this. No-fault. No-fault. It's nobody's fault. Both of us could walk away scot-free. It's over. Just like that. Like it never happened and it's not my fault or his. I should have been relieved.

"What's the rush here?" I asked. "We've been separated only what? Five or six months?"

"It has been twelve months plus one week and three days." An up-to-the-minute tally. "The rush, as you call it," he said, "is because I am leaving New York. I am moving to California," which he pronounced as Cal-ee-fornia.

"It's Cal-i-fornia. Short i." I smiled at him, which was something he did not return in kind. "Whatever," he said. "I am moving to California to live in Los Angeles. We have an office there. In Los Angeles." By *we*, Max meant Rand McNally, the company for whom he designed his maps, the people who paid him to draw lines in the sand. *We* no longer had anything to do with us, with Max and me. "If you would sign the papers now," he said, "I would be most appreciative." Max uncapped a felt-tipped pen and held it out for me to take.

"Like salmon," I said sadly as I scribbled my signature, and Max asked, "Like who? What are you saying?"

"We're like salmon." Because I could tell that he still wasn't getting it, I elaborated. "Salmon. Like you eat smoked or poached with dill sauce. Salmon. The fish. When salmon are ready to die, they return to the place of their birth. They end where they began."

"Yes," Max said. "We have come full circle," and on that spot which marked our beginning, we came to our end. There the two of us stood, feigning no memories. Like we couldn't have cared less. A pair of hypocrites, as if what I'd signed away was not my love, but something insignificant.

As I watched him walk off, I thought, "Maybe he'll come back. Maybe he'll go around the block and return to me." I waited on the corner of West Broadway and Chambers until the sun began to set, and I had to wonder to which circle of the inferno we had gone and damned ourselves.

22

elegy: Couplets consisting of a hexameter followed by a pen-
tameter line. Usually formal in tone and diction, suggested either
by the death of an actual person or by the poet's contemplation of
the tragic aspects of life. In either case, the emotion, originally ex-
pressed as a lament, finds consolation in the contemplation of
some permanent principle.

It was while standing in a
ray of morning light on a Thursday that I last called Bella. The sort
of morning light which shows itself most often in memory and in
dreams, as if from behind a gossamer curtain, and patches of this
light dappled the tree outside my window. It was Goneril who answered the phone. Twice a week, I called to see how my mother was
faring. On Sundays and Thursdays, I played the good daughter, the
dutiful daughter inquiring after her mother's health and happiness.

Having done what they could for her, the hospital—doctors and
administrators—washed their hands of my mother and they sent
her home, where, against all expectations, she blossomed like a
perennial. The way she appeared to be dying, but then she came
back to life. Often she felt very well, and she'd venture out to the
manicurist or to Manny's Wig Shop because she had a yen to be a
blonde, and another time when she wanted curls. She danced at the
Rosenberg kid's bar mitzvah despite how she couldn't stomach Gail

Rosenberg, who lived in the house next door. It was with mixed emotions that I accepted the possibility of my mother's recovery. First I feared she was going to die, and then I feared she wasn't going to die.

"Goneril," I said, "put my mother on the phone."

"May I ask who is calling please?" my idiot sister-in-law said, and I asked, "Who else calls you Goneril? It's Lila," I added because, on second thought, you never know.

"You're a little late, don't you think? No one is ever going to forgive you," she told me.

"Forgive me for what this time?" They were always mad at me, that bunch, for one reason or another.

"For what?" Goneril's pitch went way up. "You dare to ask for what?"

"Yes," I said. "I dare to ask for what. What did I do now that was so terrible?"

"You don't show up to your mother's funeral, and you have the nerve . . ." She sputtered like a biplane running out of fuel.

Bella had died on Tuesday, while I was with Leon, but no one called to tell me. No one called me to tell me that my mother was dead. Not my father or my brothers or either of the sisters-in-law or my Aunt Mitzie even, a person on whom you can usually rely to spread a story as if gossip were butter on a hot roll.

Jews, even the sort of namby-pamby Jews who change their name from Moscowitz to Morse, don't wait for the body to cool before burying it. I did not attend my mother's funeral because no one thought to let me know she died and because I called a day too late. "Someone should have called me," I said to Goneril, and she said, "That's no excuse."

My family sat *shiva* the way they did all things Jewish—American-style *shiva*, which is a half-assed hybrid between a memorial service and a Friars Club roast. If the Morse family had to identify with any group of Jews, it would be the Reform, which has more in common with the Iroquois Nation than with Orthodox Judaism. There was no trace of the Old World Jew in their grief. They sat on the couch and in armchairs, and no one sat on the floor. The mirrors were not draped with black cloth, and my father's jacket pocket was intact when it should've been torn in mourning. He and my brothers were freshly shaved, and Goneril and Regan were dolled up. Dolled up for them, that is. Neither of the stepsisters was what I'd call a snappy dresser, but they both wore lipstick and mascara and a gold bangle bracelet dangled from Regan's wrist. One bangle bracelet. Goneril had a ruby and pearl brooch pinned to her cardigan sweater.

In the dining room, spread out buffet style on the table, was an amount of food which could have fed the people of Chad. A roast beef the size of a child, two turkeys, vats of potato salad, fruit salad, cole slaw. You had your choice of rye bread, seven-grain bread, and kaiser rolls. Not to mention the tub of chicken salad, the cheddar cheese spread, and a baked ham garnished with pineapple slices and maraschino cherries.

The pig, in all its edible forms, was no stranger to the Morse household. We ate ham sandwiches for lunch, and there was always bacon on hand to complement our eggs. Also we ate shrimp and lobster and steamed clams, although we did have two sets of dishes. The good china was for company and the everyday plates, earthenware, for us when there was no one around to impress. To keep kosher may have been a mark of piety, but according to my parents, it was the way of the ignorant. Bella was fond of making the argument that if God didn't want us to mix meat and dairy, tell her why there's a McDonald's in every shopping center.

I pulled up a chair joining the circle just as Aunt Mitzie was putting the finishing touches on an amusing story about my mother. It was a story I already knew. The one about how she'd gotten locked in a bathroom stall in the Lord & Taylor's ladies' lounge. "And you know how Bella was," Mitzie said. "Rather than call for assistance and risk a scene, she came slithering out on her belly from that six-inch space between the door and the floor. Thank God she was so thin. That's all I could say."

That's what they do at these half-assed *shivas*. Eat and tell amusing stories about the deceased. Remember them fondly. Have a little laugh as a reminder that you are not dead too.

Practically on my hands and knees, I had asked Dora and Estella to come with me to sit *shiva* for my mother. "She was your niece," I said, but Estella flatly refused. "You know perfectly well that we don't go out." It's some kind of ghostly law, that apparitions don't take trains or ride in cars. That they can't take leave of their dwelling lest they risk purgatory. "Besides," Dora reminded me, "we never liked Bella."

In an attempt to be a part of this family, which was, after all, my family, I chimed in. "How about the time she came home from the A&P with an empty six-pack of Coke. Six empty cans. Apparently, it was a factory error, but still, I asked her how could she not notice. They weighed nothing. Six empty aluminum cans are light as air."

Everyone quit eating, and all eyes were on me. As if I had their undivided attention. Only it wasn't their undivided attention I had. It was their undivided indignation. Not only do I have the audacity to show my face after having missed the funeral, but then I barge in on the mourning as if I were indeed a member of the family. "The gall of you." Aunt Mitzie tightened her fingers around the fat gold chain which hung from her fat pink neck. As if she were reining in her fury.

"I think it would be better for everyone if you left," said Howard. Mitzie's son grew up to fulfill his dream. Howard is an actuary for Allstate Insurance. Waggle a piece of graph paper in front of him and Howard gets a hard-on.

It was best for them to excise me, remove me from the skin of things as if I were a wart. My presence, at this late date, distressed them. As if I marred the surface of their grief.

Before anyone had the chance to second Howard's motion, I excused myself from the inner circle and went wandering through the house.

My first thought was that they'd been robbed, such was the state of my parents' bedroom. As if, while the family was out there in the living room chowing down on roast beef sandwiches and reminiscing, a burglar came in through the bedroom window. The bureau drawers were opened and left that way. Like tongues hanging out. The night tables were overturned and closets were nearly empty. The worthless stuff—my mother's underwear and her shoes, which were no good to anyone because Bella had herself a hefty set of hooters and a dainty size six foot—were scattered in piles on the floor. Goneril and Regan had been there before me. The jewelry boxes had been eviscerated. Picked clean, and those two vultures left me not so much as one small bauble. I suppose it could be said that my mother would've wanted it that way. My mother adored Goneril and Regan both. It was that old story.

Short of genetic testing, there was never much to indicate that my mother and I were related by blood. There was no trace of my mother in my face. I had not her chestnut-colored hair, her leaning-toward-olive complexion, her wide mouth, her dark brown eyes, her 36C boobs, nor her eyesight, which was keen. Yet another thing for which she never quite forgave me. That my physiognomy is of my father's side of the family. The physical resemblance between his sister and me was manifest, except that I have not grown fat. Often my mother said to me, "My God, Lila. You are the spitting image of Mitzie." Then she would shudder. "I can't stand the sight of that woman."

I sat on the floor to sort out the cast-off items with the intent of putting them away. Away behind closed doors, because my father should not have to deal with my mother's underwear and her shoes. That would've been too sad, my father gathering up into his arms my mother's undergarments redolent of her perfume, Shalimar. Nor should he have to know that Goneril and Regan looted her personal belongings.

From a viper's nest of panty hose I untangled a black bra. Christian Dior. Silk. Bella's breasts were round and firm up until the very end. She was lucky that way. I would keep the bra for myself. Not to wear, because I'm a 34B, but as a memento. I thought maybe I would hang it on my wall or display it on a shelf. "Oh," I might have said. "That was my mother's." The way Henry says of his sterling tea set.

Setting the bra aside, I lifted another one, pink lace, and hidden under one cup, like the pea in the shell game, was a glass eye staring up at me. "Meryl," I said. I'd found Meryl, and I picked fuzz off the monkey's face. As if I were a mother monkey grooming her baby, and I cradled Meryl in my hands before bringing the toy monkey to my lips.

The strongest family tie I had, and it was with an inanimate object. A toy monkey who also was cast off, forgotten, and was something like a sister to me. I put Meryl, my legacy, in my pocket, and leaving all else behind, I slipped out the back door.

23

---

poetic license: A freedom allowed the poet to depart in subject matter, grammar, or diction from what would be proper in ordinary prose discourse, or when the poet invents fictions or takes liberties with the facts, as when Virgil makes Dido the contemporary of Aeneas.

SITTING ON PUBLIC BENCHES is something Carmen and I do well together. On benches throughout the city and over the years, she and I have shared profound and tender moments.

At Father Demo Square I say, "Let's sit," and I ease onto an Adirondack-green bench, the paint chipped and weathered from the elements. Carmen sits beside me. At our feet, pigeons bob for crumbs.

The heat, a dogged ninety-two degrees, surrounds the city like an ambush. The heat, the humidity, and the garbage work together combining forces to produce a foul smell to the air. "A thunderstorm would be good," I say, and Carmen promises, "We'll get one soon. I feel a storm coming on." Then Carmen pauses, her finger in the air like an antenna picking up sound waves. "Or maybe those are marriage vibrations I'm getting," she says. Like she is Nostradamus or Madame Blavatsky.

"Yeah?" I ask. "Who's getting married?"

"I don't know. I hope the hell it's not me. Anyway, it's probably just a storm. You know how I sometimes get those two signals crossed."

Carmen's third marriage ended but six months ago, having spanned a duration of three months and five days. Her third husband was a conceptual artist, which is a way of saying he did nothing. Other than watch television, about which he made snide comments, which were supposed to lead us to believe that he was above watching television. Her second husband drank, but at least that got him out of the house some.

Carmen lights a Pall Mall unfiltered, and she exhales through her nose as if she were a dragon lady. "Have you worked it out yet," she asks me, "about what you're going to do in September?"

"September?" I ask.

"Yes. September. As in the month following this one. It's only what, two weeks away now? What are you going to do? Are you going to teach this semester or not?"

September is only two weeks away now, and I am still waiting for a miracle to fall from the sky and into my lap. A miracle in the form of money. A prize, a grant, a cash award, a dead uncle. Enough to get by on without needing to teach for another semester at least because I need the time to finish my book. Thus far, my prayers have gone unanswered. "That's what you can give me for my birthday," I tell Carmen. "Money. Not a fortune. Ten thousand dollars would see me through."

Carmen snorts and picks a fleck of tobacco from her lower lip. She flicks it away, and the pigeons chase it down as if it were food. "You can't get blood from a stone," she says, which was one of Max's favorite expressions, only he would say, "It is not possible to get blood from a parsnip." Don't ask where he got the parsnip from because I have no idea.

The speed with which this summer has flown by is unaccountable. Not to mention how little I have accomplished in these months. I try to not think about the pages spread over my desk.

Which turns out to be like that trick where you tell children, "Whatever you do, don't think about a hippopotamus." Once warned, they can think of nothing else, and I think up another thing I'd like for my birthday. Another thing impossible. "Time," I say to Carmen. "How about buying me time?"

"How much time are you talking about?" Carmen asks as if this were doable.

"Three years," I say. No hesitation. "Three years. Rather than turning thirty-five, I want to be turning thirty-two." Thirty-five. I am not ready for the second half of my life. Not when I haven't worked out the kinks from the first half.

"Okay," Carmen says.

"Okay what? What is okay?"

"Okay, I will give you three years for your birthday," Carmen tells me, as if that were nothing special.

"And exactly how are you going to arrange for that?" I ask, disbelieving not her intent but her ability. "Only Superman can make time go backward," I say. Superman, being Superman and all that goes with the job, is able to grab hold of the earth's axis and spin it counterclockwise. By reputation, poets are thought to be elitist in the way that we don't know from the likes of Superman. But that is to misjudge us. I know of one poet who regularly steals phrases from Miss Piggy of the Muppets although, to keep the record straight, I ought to add that Miss Piggy is not given her due credit.

"Trust me on this," Carmen says. "Three years less is no problem. Consider it a done deal."

Carmen and I have been friends for seventeen years, and not that I believe that she can make me three years younger, but I play along because it's something we do. "To make adjustments for my impending change in age, other numbers need to be recalculated," I say. "For example, I know it seems longer but we go back only fourteen years together." Also, I inform Carmen that she will be two and a half years older than me instead of how she used to be six months younger.

"I'm not sure if I like this." Carmen sounds as if she's having second thoughts, but she is not. Carmen is far more concerned with what will happen than with that which has already occurred. Here I am looking to roll back the calendar while Carmen fast-forwards time to the spot where it runs out. "You do realize," she says to me, "that one of us will die before the other. Either I'm going to have to see to your funeral arrangements or you're going to have to see to mine."

If Carmen is going to be the one to make my funeral arrangements, it is likely that I will first rot and turn to dust in the spot where she found me. Maybe in the bathtub or slumped in a chair. Carmen is not always reliable about practical matters. If I were to ask Carmen to water my plants while I was away on vacation, odds are I would return to a dead hibiscus and a drooping dewberry in potted soil as dry as bone. That is if I had any plants, which I don't because plants require commitment. One of the many reasons I love Carmen is this element of surprise.

"I refuse to discuss such things," I tell her. "Here I am barely thirty-two years old and you're talking about my funeral."

"Maybe it will be my funeral first," she says, "seeing that I'm soon to be the elder now."

"No." I tell her that can't be. "I have no experience with funerals. I wouldn't know what to do."

Carmen has another thought. "Maybe we'll go together. In a plane crash." Carmen brightens with the comfort that thought brings, and the storm clouds gather and the sky goes black.

Thunder cracks, and the rain comes fast and furious. The trees bend with the wind as if they are trying to hold on to their leaves, but the leaves are swept along the streets, and in no time flat Carmen and I look like a pair of drowned cats. It feels nice, this rain. It's cool and clean, and turning toward the heavens Carmen says, "Okay, so maybe it wasn't a marriage coming on."

24

occasionals: Any poem, light or serious, good or bad, written for a special occasion and with a special purpose, as, for example, memorial pieces, birthday odes, tributes to a poet; public poetry which has a practical social function to perform.

BECAUSE THE MIRACLE HAS YET to happen and it looks as if I'm going to have to teach this coming semester after all, I'm stuck here grinding out a course outline for a master class called, unimaginatively enough, "Poetry Writing II." I came up with the title myself. Master class means only that you need to have completed the prerequisite of Poetry Writing I.

The phone rings, and I am grateful to be taken away from the task at hand. It is Henry calling, and at that, Dora and Estella start knocking about in the bedroom like they're looking for something lost. Drawers open and shut, papers rustle, a shoe falls, and I shhh them. Call it happenstance, but Dora and Estella make a racket whenever it is Henry on the phone. Easily, I could get the impression that they don't like him much more than they liked Max. Or it could be something more sinister. Maybe my ghosts want me to be alone, that if I were to share my life with another living soul, they might be displaced. As if they fear I would need them no longer.

Henry has called to ask what I would want for a birthday gift. "Give me a hint," he says.

"Something pawnable," I tell Henry. "Pawnable and trans-portable. Precious stones and metals," I clarify.

"Why is it," Henry wants to know, "that Jewish women have a lust for jewelry? Is it the spelling? The J-E-W connection?" Henry thinks he is onto something big, and it could be that this is the sort of mind-set which has turned Dora and Estella against him.

"Henry," I say, "don't be a moron here. What? You've forgotten your history of the world? The Inquisition. Pogroms. Nazis. That sort of event. When the authorities come knocking at our door to tell us we've got two minutes to pack what we can and get out, we can't very well put a piano in our brassieres."

"Aren't you forgetting that this is America?" Henry says. "Things like that don't happen here," to which I say, "Hah! Tell that to the Oneontas." Then I issue Henry a warning. "Whatever you do," I say, "don't get me flowers or chocolates. I don't appreciate perishables of any kind."

In addition to flowers and chocolates, there are other items for which I would express little gratitude. Do not expect me to gush when I unwrap a coffee bean grinder, a salad shooter, a label maker, or scented soaps. And forget the cutesy-wootsy stuff. Plastic stat-uettes of urchins, arms outstretched, on platforms inscribed "I LOVE YOU THIS MUCH!"

"So," Henry says, "for your birthday, you want me to buy you jewelry to sew into the lining of your underwear in case you need to flee from the Germans." Because I've told him next to nothing about my marriage to Max, Henry thinks this is funny.

I fled from Max with my possessions stuffed into one brown pa-per bag. Which was all I brought with me because while married to Max, I had no need for material goods like clothes or dishes. Also, the paucity of possessions made for easier leaving. I would've pre-ferred a plastic bag with handles, but we did not have any of that kind. Max eschewed plastic and other environmental hazards.

Running away from home with a brown paper bag in tow was how I did it when I was a child, packing up my best toys and announcing to my family, "I'm running away because no one loves me." Despite the sincerity of my intentions, I never got beyond the front porch, where I would sit and wait for my parents to grow sick with fear and come looking for me. Eventually, I would grow bored out there or else the night would make shadows and noises that were the sounds of bats and murderers.

At the supermarket, like he was a devotee of Rachel Carson, Max unfailingly requested brown bags, and whenever he received a delivery in a box with Styrofoam peanuts, it was returned to sender without delay. "I do not accept those Styrofoam potatoes," Max said.

"Peanuts," I told him. "We call them peanuts."

"Whatever you call them, they are an insult to the environment."

He got no argument from me on that score, although I found his environmentalist stance perplexing because, except for the park, Max seemed to have no use for nature other than as points and guidelines on a map. The oceans and rivers and mountain ranges were but boundaries. Where one place stopped being and another began. Where, on the map, the lettering changed from Roman style for nations to italic for lakes and the seas and to Gothic for mountains and valleys. Whenever I stopped to admire a bird, which did not happen often because I'm no nature nut either, Max made noises of exasperation and tapped his foot the way you do when you're stuck on a long line at the bank. Also, Max blamed dogs for shitting on the sidewalk.

"It's hardly the dogs' fault," I argued on the dogs' behalf. "It's the people who don't clean up after their dogs. They're the ones you ought to be cursing. Dogs don't know from toilets," I said, but Max continued to point the finger of accusation at the dachshunds, the golden retrievers, and especially at the cross-breeds. Which I considered to be nefarious scapegoating on his part. Which I considered to be a cultural trait.

I left Max on a Monday morning shortly after he left for work, and after I sprayed Lysol in the bedroom to obliterate all traces of my perfume and my scent, and after I sat at the table to write Max a note. "Dear Max, Please forgive me," and I stopped there because Max was never going to forgive me. Why bother asking for what you'll never get? Not to mention I probably would never forgive myself either.

My underwear, which was dirty, went into the brown bag first. On top of the bras, panties, stockings, and garter belts I put my books and notebooks, and then, like the strata of the earth, came my incidentals. Toothbrush, hairclips, tampons, Oil of Olay. Everything I had brought to my marriage and everything I was taking away from it fit into one brown paper bag like nineteen dollars' worth of groceries.

Yet Henry scoffs at the notion that you never know when you'll need to flee, when you'll want everything you own that is of value to fit into one bag. That history, of course, happens again and again, and that is why I ask him for items pawnable and transportable.

25

....

monorhyme: a passage in a poem, or a strophe, or an entire poem in which all lines have the same end rhyme. It is often used capriciously as an artificial device for producing satirical or comical effects.

THE WAY THE LOCALS LIVING IN werewolf territory tend to grow apprehensive with the coming of the full moon, my impending birthday is making everyone nervous. Including Leon.

"Do you think you could treat it like it was any other day?" Leon asks me. "Some people are able to do that. Go to work, come home, have dinner, watch a little television, read a book, go to bed. No big deal."

"Yeah, sure," I say. "Try asking a Catholic to blow off Christmas."

"Christmas," Leon observes, "is a day of worship," and I say, "Right. My point exactly."

My birthday is the holiday in celebration of myself. The only one that is for me alone. My day, and that is something big. Three and four months in advance, my mother would call me over to her side, and together we set the birthday ball in motion. First we would pick a theme around which we selected the menu, the party favors, related games and prizes. Take the year I turned six. The Cat in the Hat party. I adored *The Cat in the Hat*. Not to mention the influence it had on me. Those *abcb* rhyme schemes, the iamb joined to the anapest, the Skeltonic verse elevating parallelism to a major rhetorical element. It's good stuff.

"Some poets," I tell Leon as an aside, "are liars about that sort of thing, their early influences. You wouldn't believe it. They'll look you straight in the face and claim that, as children, they were reading Tennyson or H.D. Oh, and Blake. Always Blake. Yeah, right. Well, fuck them. I was reading *The Cat in the Hat,* and I'm the poet with the two-page spread in *People* magazine."

"You don't have to convince me of your stature as a poet," Leon says, and I am grateful to Leon, that with him I don't have to prove myself.

The party hats were replicas of the cat's hat. Red-and-white stripes and stovepipe. We had kitty cupcakes and played Pin-the-Goldfish-in-the-Teacup, and the prize was a real live goldfish in a glass bowl. Like Henry's goldfish. I pinned the paper goldfish in the teacup first, before anybody else, which meant I did win the game. The goldfish in the bowl should have been mine, but my mother said no. I wasn't allowed to have the prize because it was my party, and she had some rule about that, about how the hostess couldn't win the goldfish. I had a fit. Injustice never sat well with me, and graciousness has always been an effort. Alicia Braverman got the goldfish, and each child went home with their own copy of the book and the spin-off toys.

"That's something," Leon concedes, and I say, "I was known for having the most swank birthday parties in the neighborhood, which was no mean feat given where I grew up."

Right up until the sweet sixteen debacle, I was not to be outdone. The same year that Stacy Goldstein had a miniature golf party and Marcy Seldon's father took her and twelve of her best friends to Palisades Amusement Park, I had a bowling party which was catered by Twin Lanes. Our Coca-Colas were served in glassware shaped like bowling pins. Each girl was given a small bowling bag which could also be used as a purse, and it was filled with candy.

Good candy, too. Snickers and M&M's and Baby Ruths and no butterscotch candies which everybody hated. My tenth birthday party was a divine affair except for the part where I bowled a zero. With each frame, my visions of spares and strikes went kerplunk as the ball rolled in slow motion down the gutter. I hit no pins whatever. I bowled a zero, and those little shits who were my guests, and therefore were supposed to clamor to be my best friend because that was birthday party protocol, called me a spastic. It was my birthday. They should have been nice to me on my birthday.

"You had expectations which were not met," Leon says. "Expectations that could never be met. You set yourself up for disappointment."

"I didn't set myself up for disappointment. I got set up for disappointment. Every year, there was a set-up."

"Every year?" Leon scoffs. As if he doesn't believe me. As if I were being hyperbolic here, and I say, "Go ahead. Pick a year. Any year."

"Okay," Leon says. "Eight."

"Eight. I invited the new girl in school to my birthday party. Which," I add, "was very generous of me because I barely knew her."

She arrived at my house for the party, and in that instant I fell in love with her because she forked over a gift that was wrapped by someone near to God. The angel Gabriel or whoever it was that made Joseph's coat of many colors. Never before had I seen a package wrapped in such perfection. Pink and purple and blue tissue paper was layered to look like summer's dusk. Attached to the purple moiré ribbon with silver threads were pink flowers crafted by magic or a great artisan. I dared not to venture a guess as to what magnificence this box contained.

Throughout the afternoon, for the duration of rounds of Musical Chairs and Simon Says and Twister, I eyeballed that box. My ears nearly popped with desire before my mother allowed that it was time for cake and ice cream and the ceremonial opening of the gifts.

It was my habit to turn my piece of cake upside-down, to save the frosting, the best part, for last. In that same way, I opened all the other gifts as if they were foreplay. Trinkets nice enough in and of themselves, but still a prelude. Bridesmaids come down the aisle before the bride does, and some group you never heard of opens for U-2. I tore away the wrapping, hastily ripping into shreds the paper of summer's dusk. Inside the box, under a layer of white tissue paper, was a white polo shirt. I had a dozen white polo shirts in my chest of drawers but even if I'd had none, a white polo shirt could never be a fancy thing imagined. "You tricked me." I turned on the girl who, only hours before, had won my heart unwaveringly. "You tricked me." I flung the shirt to the floor and kicked it across the room, which was hateful of me. I know that now. Certainly, the girl wanted me to be pleased with the white shirt, to love it even. To lift it from the box and feel the fabric against my cheek. She must have felt awful, but I didn't stop to consider her when I kicked it again, whereupon my mother banished me from my own party. I was to stay in my bedroom until I was ready to come back downstairs and apologize to that deceitful girl, which I would not do. Now, as I relate this episode to Leon, I remember that the girl cried. I made her cry, and I blink twice to push the image away. Nonetheless, I see her chin quivering.

"What did you want there to be in the box?" Leon asks me. "What were you expecting?"

I can't answer him. I want to answer him, but I have that same sense of frustration as when I try to write about love, the groping in the air to catch the imagination. I have no answer, but Leon refuses to accept my silence. "Take a guess," he says. "A wild guess."

"A unicorn," I say. "I was expecting a unicorn to be in the box, to flutter its wings and fly around the room before coming to rest on my shoulder," and Leon nods as if my answer were the right one. "So," he asks, "what do you have planned for your birthday coming up?"

"Nothing definite yet," I tell him. "The night before, the birthday eve, I have a reading to give. At the library. Henry's been after me to think of something I'd like to do, but that's his responsibility.

Mostly I'm waiting to see what happens with Carmen and the business of my age. If I'm younger, I might have other plans altogether. You know how youth is fickle."

"Lila." Leon leans forward. "You're doing it again. Setting yourself up for disappointment. You can't go back in time, Lila. Time is not going to run counterclockwise just for you."

To placate Leon, I say I know that, but just because something has never happened before doesn't mean it isn't going to happen now. As Max would've said, "This is the first time for everything."

26

encomium: A Greek choral poem in celebration not of a god but of a hero, sung at the *komos*, the jubilant or reveling procession which celebrated the victor in the games; a rhetorical exercise exalting the virtues of some legendary figure or praising the extraordinary deeds of a human being.

THERE IS A FIRST TIME FOR everything, and the first and only time I fell in love it was with Max. Which is somewhat remarkable given I was past thirty years old and had yet to have a dry season. But love? True love? Great love? No. Love, capital *L*, heart-shaped *O*, arrow piercing the *V* to drip blood over the *E*, the kind of love that, more often than not, makes a mess of your life, was not something I knew firsthand. Before I met Max no one had gotten the best of me. As if the best of me were something to thieve. I was like the New Yorker who claims, "Twenty-six years in this city and I've never been mugged," or the owner of a high-priced automobile who swats the fender and puffs out his chest to brag, "One hundred and seventy-two thousand miles on this baby without a hitch." Like that, I was known to boast, "Thirty-one years old and I've never been in love." As if falling in love were the same thing as falling on a patch of ice. A clumsy move that is sure to leave an unsightly bruise.

A hollow boast—*I've never been in love*—because I wanted it to happen. So much I wanted it to happen that I dared not mouth the words. The way old Jews look down at a newborn baby and declare it to be ugly and stupid, so as to keep away the angels of death, angels who might be tempted to snatch a beautiful and brilliant child for themselves. I dared not ask for love because who knows what you could get instead.

It happened when I wasn't looking. When my eyes were shut tight, but I knew it was love with Max, my love, when in his bed and at the exact moment when I thought to myself, "No, it's not possible," but there it came. I fell in love on the slide of yet another orgasm like the rolling hills of a Wisconsin dairy farm. Creamy too. The way I loved Max, the way he loved me, there should've been a law against it. Actually, there was a law against it although technically it was no longer enforced.

During that same romantic interlude, Max had something like a seizure. When it was over, he said, "Now I understand why *rassenschande* was forbidden."

"*Rassen* what? What is that word?" I asked, and Max translated. "*Rassenschande.* The mingling of the races."

Near the end of the war, Max's father was sent to fight at the Russian front where he was wounded in the leg, which rendered him a gimp for glory of the Third Reich. His mother, with pride and possibly there was some kind of erotic aspect going on as well, wore the uniform of that organization which was similar to the Campfire Girls, only they had Hitler for a scoutmaster. As if that was not enough to live with, Max's family had to bear the weight of Albert Speer. Uncle Albert. A blood relative on his mother's side.

"This is not to excuse him," Max said, "but Albert Speer was not as terrible as the rest of them. He did not know everything that was going on. He was ignorant of the final solution, and when he learned what they had done, he asked to be punished."

"Is that so?" I said, and Max said, "Yes. It is so."

"Well then." I propped myself up on one elbow. "How would you like to buy a bridge in Brooklyn?"

"I am not following you," Max said. "What does a bridge for sale have to do with Speer's ignorance? Where, please, is the connection?"

"The connection," I explained, "is your gullibility. That perhaps you are easily duped."

"Duped," Max said. "This is a word I do not know. What does this duped mean?"

Leaning in, I kissed his eyes as if I were the undertaker putting pennies there, and I said, "Do you know how many relatives I lost in the Holocaust?"

Max dropped his gaze in shame. "Oh," he said. "Must we open this book of worms?"

"It's *can* of worms," I told him, "and we opened it with our first kiss."

"This is very difficult for me, Lila. Our fathers' sins are upon us greatly." Max said he was so sorry and I said, "Duped again," because unless you're talking tribe as family, I lost no one that way, and next I experienced a rush of love for Max like I was on a whirligig gone out of control.

"Let me ask you this," I wanted to know. "If everyone loathes the Germans, who do the Germans loathe?"

"The Swiss," Max said, not missing a beat.

"The Swiss? The Dairy Queen of the Alps? The people who brought us hot chocolate and numbered bank accounts?" We did not yet know about the Swiss, safeguarding and then refusing to return, ill-begotten gains. "Who," I asked, "could hate Heidi and the little Swiss goats?"

"The Germans," Max said, and then he told me about the Swiss girlfriend he had. "When I was a university student, I dated a big, strapping Swiss girl with long blond braids and ruddy cheeks. Whenever she had an orgasm, she would shudder from head to toe and then she would say, 'I hate when that happens.' "

If Max and I were the prototypes, it was no wonder that this mingling of the races was forbidden. If, back then, German men and Jewish women had gone at it the way Max and I did, the history books would be in need of serious rewrites. Decades ahead of its time you would've had the slogan "Make Love, Not War!" Rather than snapping to attention with a "Heil Hitler," the men of Germany would've waved a hand and said, "Get lost. I'm busy." The National Socialists would never have been able to mobilize an army willing to leave their beds and their loved ones. Oh, and what parades there would have been! Forget goose-stepping with rifles and bayonets. What we would have had was row upon row of German men, marching with their pants unzipped and their cocks waving high like flags. There you had the glory of the Fatherland. Like that, they could've ruled the world.

Because I didn't come up with such an image from nowhere, and because it is worth noting, let me make mention here of Max's cock. Oh, where to begin to expound on its splendors! Statuesque. Like chiseled from marble. Magnificent to behold, and in this assessment I am including the foreskin, which was an item I had previously found to be as appealing as a sheep's intestines. Also, I was never quite sure what to do with a foreskin—how to handle it—until Max showed me the way to peel it back to reveal the fruit more perfect even than the banana.

And not only was it gorgeous in form, but oh! how it functioned. Like a Mercedes Benz, a Krups coffee machine, a cuckoo clock. A solid example of German engineering. With the purr of a pussycat, it started up with the press of a button, a kiss on the neck, the touch of a hand, a gaze across the room, a smile, a thought, and it never, ever broke down. Time after time and again and again, Max got hard on a wish. Plus, you'd think by the fourth or fifth go-round on any given night, he'd be blasting off with nothing save for hot air, but you'd be thinking wrong. As reliable as a geyser, and he was like a prize cow in terms of significant output. A gob of jizz that mingled with my juice as his sweat mingled with my sweat as his tongue mingled with my tongue as our mouths and arms and fingers and toes mingled in the name of love. Oh, *rassenschande.* Sweet *rassenschande.*

It is likely that our evocation of *rassenschande* was nothing more than a gimmick Max and I cooked up. To enhance the excitement. The extra kick afforded by that which is illicit. As if neither of us were able to trust our love for what it was. But a generation ago, we would've been jailed for it. Or worse, and although it was no longer forbidden by anyone but some old ghosts and hold-outs, still I did my time for *rassenschande.*

27

clerihew: Consists of two couplets of unequal length often with complex or somewhat ridiculous rhymes and presents a potted biography. The humor consists in concentrating on the trivial, the fantastic, or the ridiculous and presenting it with dead-pan solemnity as the characteristic, the significant, or the essential.

"IN THE REFRIGERATOR," HENRY tells me, "there is a bottle of Chablis."

We're that way now, Henry and me. That I help myself to food and drink from his kitchen, and he urinates with the bathroom door ajar. I'd like to write a poem about that, about the death of something due to peeing with the bathroom door open. A coronach, which is a lament, in quantitative accentual-syllabics. Of course, I'd like to write a poem on any subject in any form, but that's not happening.

While reaching for the wineglasses, I look in on the goldfish. Weeks ago Henry moved the fish into the soup tureen because it had outgrown the salad bowl. It is an unusual fish insofar as it is still alive. Goldfish, those that live in salad bowls and have regular exposure to children, rarely have a life span that exceeds two or three days. Often they go belly-up in a matter of hours. This goldfish, however, has been around for months and months, and it is dancing its fan dance. Its mouth makes those kissing movements for which fish are famous. "Oh," I say to the fish, "you're hungry, aren't you, little fishie?"

I nose around looking for the fish food, and I find it in a cut-crystal salt dish between the coffee canister and the sugar bowl. I drop a pinch into the soup tureen, and the fish tracks down and devours each flake. "You want more?" I ask the fish and I give it two pinches this time, and Henry calls out to me, "Don't overfeed the fish."

Carrying two glasses of wine, I return to Henry. We kiss, and then he makes mention how I've poured the wine into goblets meant for red wine, not white. "Does it really matter?" I ask because I would like to go on kissing without interruption.

"It doesn't really matter," Henry says, "but it sort of matters." The fact is Henry can't bear drinking white wine from a red-wine glass. His kisses are halfhearted and inattentive, and then he gets up from the couch. "I'll just pour this into the other goblets," he says and takes the two glasses of wine with him into the kitchen.

Henry is taking his sweet time. My foot taps a restless tune of impatience when he calls out to me, "Lila. Come here a minute, would you."

Henry is peering into the soup tureen, and he steps aside for me to look too. "Something is wrong with the fish," he says, and he is right. It is on the floor of the tureen, and it is motionless. Its gills open and close slowly and with what seems to be tremendous effort.

"It was fine a few minutes ago. Dancing up a storm, and it ate all the food. Maybe it's just digesting a big meal."

"How much food did you give it?" Henry's tone is accusatory.

"A couple of pinches," I say.

"Pinches? How much is a pinch?"

"Like this." I go to the cut-crystal salt dish and take the flakes between my fingers to show Henry what is meant by a pinch.

"Is that what you fed the fish? Lila," Henry says. "that's not fish food. That's plant food."

"Oh," I say. "Is there a difference?"

Plant food is made up of nitrogen, phosphoric acid, ammonium, and potassium nitrates. Chemicals which are good for plants, but poison for fish. "The fish food I keep up here." Henry goes to the cabinet overhead and gets out a shaker that is clearly labeled fish food.

The fish is leaning sideways and I shout at Henry, "Do something!"

"What? What can I do?" Henry is at a loss, and I'm shaking all over at what I have done. "I don't know," I say. "Call the animal hospital. Maybe we can take it to the emergency room."

Henry rummages through his cabinets for a Tupperware tub so that we can safely transport the fish without spilling the water while I stand over the tureen and coach. "Come on, fish," I say. "Get better. You can do it. Sit up straight now. Come on, get better. Please get better. Whatever you do, fish, don't die on me. Please don't die on me," I beg it to not die on me, and then it does.

I run from the kitchen and throw myself facedown on the couch. I put my hands over my ears as if to shut out the voice of my conscience, and I hear the flush of the toilet. I feel sort of sick. That awful sickness which comes with damage that is irreparable. You know there is no going back to fix things which are all your doing, and Henry comes and sits beside me. He pats my back, and he says, "Come on now. It was an accident, and what's done is done." Or as Max would have said, "There's no use sweeping up spilled milk."

Sitting up, I ask, "That was the fish? You flushed the fish down the toilet?"

"Yes," Henry tells me. "He got a New York funeral."

I nod, as if to say I expected as much, but I was also expecting to learn that he put the fish in a shoe box alongside his parents. I often suppose that someday Henry will have his closet filled with shoe boxes the way Imelda Marcos did. Only instead of patent leather pumps and Manolo Blahnik sandals, Henry's shoe boxes will contain the remains all of those whom he loved.

28

passion play: Two brief Latin plays from the *Carmina Burana* manuscript (13th century) indicate that the verse of the Passion proper was invented as prologue to the Resurrection. Quickly becoming more popular than the Resurrection, the play continues to be acted. However, it has been recast on the lines of classical drama.

I LIKE TO THINK THAT WAS A difference between Max and me. Our approach to spilled milk. I like thinking that I'd have gotten out the broom and tried to save what I could of it. I like to think that, but it's a delusion because when the milk spills, I'm the type who steps in it and says, "What milk? I don't see any milk." Still, I continue to maintain that if Max had left me, as opposed to the other way around, I wouldn't have let him go. I would have tracked him down, chased after him, clung to his ankles, and begged him to return to me. I would've chained myself to his door and camped out on the welcome mat until he agreed to let me in. That is the sort of thing I maintain, which is a kind of self-aggrandizing. I perpetrate the mythology about myself, that I go to all lengths. I say it. Just as I say of Max that he simply let me go. That his pride meant more to him than I did. As if he were above it all, Max stood on ceremony the way Jesus stood on water. I say that about him, but deny it when referring to myself.

The fact was that, each for reasons of our own, neither of us made any attempt to learn if we could salvage the wreck. After I left Max, I never called him, I never wrote him a letter or sent a postcard. I declared him to be among the dead, and I never saw him again except when I signed the divorce papers. Carmen ran into him once and she said, "Why don't you give Lila a call? She misses you," to which Max said, "Lila cut off her nose despite her face."

"It's *to spite* her face," Carmen told him, and Max said, "Whatever. She did it, and it is done."

What's done is done then. You cannot paste together a face to its nose cut off and you cannot resurrect a dead fish. However, you can make reparations. To compensate for having killed their goldfish, I take Henry's children to Toys "R" Us, where they run roughshod over me.

Eczema's response to the fish's demise was one of neutral dispassion. "The fish is dead," she said, and then she asked if she could have an Oreo, to which Henry said, "She's just like her mother."

Polyp, however, was awash with grief. Polyp wept, "My fish. My poor fishie," and I was burdened with the knowledge that not only was I responsible for the fish's death, but that it suffered before it died.

As a result, I drop big money at Toys "R" Us, as if paying damages will do something for me. Alleviate the guilt by way of restitution to Polyp and Eczema. Certainly the two shopping bags filled with Space Invaders, G.I. Joe, Barbie, Barbie outfits, Terminators, transformers, and Polly Pockets will do nothing to help the fish. For the fish, it is too late.

With Polyp and Eczema each *schlepping* their own shopping bag, we make our way to Ray's to get a pizza to bring back to Henry's apartment because that is the plan. While we were at Toys "R" Us, Henry went to Pet Depot to buy a replacement fish, which will be a surprise for the children.

We sit at a table, and I order a large pie to go and a round of Coca-Colas for while we wait. Eczema empties the salt shaker onto the table and makes designs with the grains. Meanwhile, having, in no time flat, stripped the fatigues off G.I. Joe, Polyp takes his sister's Barbie from the bag and peels her bathing suit down to her ankles. He rubs the two dolls together until he's got G.I. Joe's face in Barbie's snatch. "Look, Lila." He wants me to see how G.I. Joe goes down on Barbie, and I say, "Very nice. That's lovely."

In a gender-defying episode, Barbie is reaming G.I. Joe when Eczema spills her soda. Coca-Cola spreads across the table and onto her lap. While I'm mopping it up with a wad of napkins, Eczema reaches over and cops a feel. She squeezes my breast as if she expects it to honk. Spreading herself out in a fan of giggles, she tells me, "You have chests."

"Yes," I concur. "I have chests. A respectable pair of chests."

"Why?" Eczema is at that stage of life. The *why* stage, which can get on your nerves because so rarely can your answer suffice.

"All women have chests," I explain. "When girls reach a certain age, their breasts develop and grow big."

Eczema shakes her head. Her blond hair whips from side to side. "No," she says. "My mommy is old, and she doesn't have chests."

"Mommy's flat," Polyp confirms.

"I want chests like Lila." Eczema gears up for a tantrum. Her face scrunches and goes red with frustration. Like she's figured out the essence of genetics and understands that the odds of a healthy pair of hooters are against her. "I want chests the same as Lila."

"Oh, calm down," I tell her. "If you want chests like mine, you can have chests like mine. What is not endowed from God, you can always get from the cosmetic surgeon." The fact is we can have whatever we want if we're willing to compromise, to accept substitutions for the real thing. "When we get back to your father's place, tell him you want implants."

"What are implants?" Polyp's got Barbie and G.I. Joe grinding butt to butt, which is a new one on me.

"Women whose breasts don't grow as big as they'd like them to grow can go to the cosmetic surgeon and get fake ones put in," I tell him. "We call those implants. They're fake breasts but they look and behave more or less like real ones."

Our pizza is ready, and I balance the box with one hand and my hip in order to hold on to Eczema, who has a predilection for running out into traffic.

Henry stands in the doorway to greet us upon our return. "Daddy!" Eczema shouts, "Inflants. I want inflants," and Henry wants to know, "Inflants? What are inflants?"

"Implants," I put the pizza down on the table. "Breast implants," I tell him. "Your daughter wants big tits," and Polyp wants to know, "Daddy, is my fish still dead?"

"Go see for yourself," Henry tells him. "Look in the kitchen. On the countertop." Henry has the new fish all set up in the salad bowl. The children dash off to witness the second coming, and Henry and I, taking advantage of the moment alone, smooch and grope a little.

Nowhere near the hot time Barbie and G.I. Joe had, but still it's pleasant touching until we are stopped by Polyp tugging on Henry's shirtsleeve. "That's not my fish," Polyp says. "That's some other fish. It's not my fish. I want my fish."

Henry kneels down to tell Polyp, "Your fish is in fish heaven."

"Which," I add, "is a very nice place for a fish to be. It's like a big blue swimming pool in Beverly Hills."

"I want my fish," Polyp cries.

"I'm sorry," Henry says. "Your fish has to stay in fish heaven. But now you have this new fish, and you can love this new fish just as much. Maybe even more."

"No," Polyp says. "Never."

"You can try," Henry says as if love were merely a matter of effort.

"This fish has a crummy tail. It's all skinny." Polyp knows that, try as the new fish might to win his affections, there is no replacing your first love and there is no deceiving the heart.

29

poète maudit: A phrase that mirrors the widening gulf in 19th-century France between the gifted poet and the public upon which his survival depends.

"HOW ARE YOU TODAY?" LEON asks, and I say, "I'm fine. You, on the other hand, are looking a bit frumpy. You could use a makeover."

Leon pulls at the hem of his skirt and says, "I am not a cabaret act, Lila. My clothes are work appropriate."

Yet another way in which Leon does not resemble your typical New York psychologist is that we're nearly at the end of August, and still Leon continues to keep his regular hours. He takes his month off in February. To go where, I do not know. Leon, in many respects, does not run with the pack.

"Maybe a little eyeshadow," I say. "Nothing garish. Just a touch in a smoky gray or aubergine."

Leon shakes his head. Also, he holds a different opinion from mine as to the reasons behind my desire to repeat ages thirty-two through thirty-five. I contend that it stems from nothing more than petty vanity. "Face it, Leon. We live in a youth-oriented culture. The younger the better, but if you must plumb the depths of my subconscious, I might own up to a fear of death." Which is an easy one to cop to because who amongst us doesn't have a fear of death?

Leon, however, thinks it has other significance, but that is Leon's job. To find significance where perhaps there might not be any. "Tell me," he says. "Where were you three years ago?"

"Where was I? As in where was I on the afternoon of August twenty-first or twenty-second or whatever day this is? Are you asking if I have an alibi? Probably right where I am now. Sitting on your couch," I say, which is a bold-faced prevarication. We both know that I first came to Leon two, not three, years ago. After a somewhat lengthy phone conversation where I told Leon a little bit about myself, about how I was experiencing fits of uncontrollable anger, that I had grown rude to the point of boorish, and I was unable to work on my book without having the dry heaves. You could say I haven't made a lot of progress. It was during that same conversation that Leon filled me in on where he went to school, where he did his training, and his approach to therapy. "Also you should know," he said, "I'm a man who wears women's clothes."

Now Leon gives me one of those looks. One of those looks that says cut the crap, so I do. "Okay," I say. "Three years ago I was in Washington Heights. With Max. Three years ago, I was married to Max."

"Yes." Leon seems excited by this. As if it were a revelation. As if we've decoded a cryptographic message or invented the lightbulb. As if we have pulled back the curtain and revealed the wizard to be a skeleton dancing in my closet. "And what else?" he asks. With enthusiasm.

I know for what Leon is fishing, and—what the hell—if it makes him happy, I can give it to him. "Three years ago," I say, "my mother was alive and well, and three years ago I was nearly done with a book that still is not finished."

"Exactly." Leon crosses his arms over his padded bosom. "You're wishing to return to the time when you were married, and your mother was still available to you, and you had better control over your work."

"My mother was never available to me." I remind Leon of all

that we'd covered in our early sessions. The tantrums, the inconsolable weeping, the rage which could only be characterized as infantile, the insatiable need to be loved, the inability to love for fear I would lose it. The blame for all of which Leon placed neatly on my mother's lap. Which, in turn, bore out Bella's theory as to why psychologists were up to no good. She'd warned me against their evil ways. "They blame the mother for everything. World War Two," she said, "Hitler's mother. If you listen to the psychologists, it was all her doing."

Because I was capable of snot-nosed immaturity well beyond the accepted time frame for that type of behavior, I told her about Leon. About how I go to a psychologist every Tuesday, about how it is his opinion that I never got enough love and attention, that I never properly bonded and was likely to have been bottle-fed.

What I didn't tell my mother was that Leon wears dresses.

"So," Leon asks me now, "what do you make of this wish of yours?"

I tell Leon that I don't make anything of any of it. "Isn't that what I pay you for?" I say. "For you to make something of it?"

"I think you are attempting to resolve some issues. I think you have unfinished business from that time in your life which you are seeking to relive now in order to resolve it. You are after closure," Leon says, and I retreat the way a skunk does. I lift my tail and emit a foul odor. "You know, Leon," I say, "sometimes you sound like a self-help book written for the general audience."

Leon and I sit in the silence that is the fallout until I clear my throat and I say, "I picked to go back three years because one or two years is hardly enough to be bothered with and four or five years might be stretching credibility. That is the whole of the reason. It has nothing to do with my mother or with Max or seeking closure," I say.

Closure. It seems to me that all I've got is closure. Like every door to every facet of my life has slammed shut in my face. Or I pull it closed behind my back. Locking myself in or out, from one empty space to another. Everything has been decided. The rhythms of the words have a predetermined order. The lines have been phrased, and the punctuation is terminal. My mother is dead and there were no final-hour confessions of regret, no apologies, and she never said "I love you" to me and I never said it to her, and Max is gone somewhere in California and I let him go, and there were no prayers to be answered. All of us carried our stupidities to the very end. How's that for closure?

Leon nods and he says, "I want to stop here. I know our time is not up but I need to talk with you about something."

I wonder if Leon is going to ask me for some advice on fashion. Tips and pointers, and I would definitely urge him to wear red, but instead he says, "I'm closing down my practice, Lila. I don't want to, but I have to take care of myself now. I have AIDS," he says, and all I can say is "When did you find out?" I can't say anything else. I ought to, but I can't.

"I've been HIV positive for seven years," he is telling me. Now he is telling me. "I've been one of the lucky ones so far, but my T-cell count has dropped dramatically. It's going to be a battle from here on in."

Now he is telling me, and all I can say is, "Why didn't you tell me when I first came to you? Two years ago, you knew. Why didn't you tell me then that you were positive? Right away on the phone you told me that you wear dresses. Why didn't you tell me this?" He has AIDS, and I am furious with him. For not telling me. For letting me come here week after week, in the dark, where I got attached to him. I am furious with him because it's over. Leon is leaving me, and I am angry with him for that. So angry that I can't express my concern for him and his health, and I can't manage to tell him that I adore him and that I need him and I can't see straight. There are noises in my head and they are messing with my vision.

"Would it have made a difference," Leon asks, "if you knew from the beginning?" and I tell him the truth. "I don't know, but you should have told me."

"You're right about that, and I am sorry. Really, Lila. Very sorry. I think I was in denial for a long time. I think that when I didn't get sick early on into the diagnosis, I started to believe that I never would."

I don't want to hear any excuses. I don't want to hear any of it. "It's not right. I have feelings for you. Deep feelings," I say.

"Lila, I'm sorry," Leon says, and I know he is. Only I don't care that he is sorry. It's very horrible but I can think only of myself, of my needs, of my loss. I should be ashamed that I cannot comfort Leon now, but to know such a thing and to act on it are not one and the same.

Leon is telling me that I can call him anytime I want to, and that he has a list of therapists for me, all of whom he highly recommends, but I'm not paying attention. I'm in a kind of shock. Something like anaphylactic shock, where my throat is swelling up on me and that is all I can think about, this swelling in my throat.

"Lila," Leon reaches out to take my hand, but I can't let him touch me. If Leon were to take my hand in his, I would be unable to let go. Rather than allow that to happen, I get up and I leave and I slam shut yet one more door behind me.

30

....

flyting: A poetical invective in which two poets assail each other alternately with scurrilous, abusive verse.

DURING THE NIGHT, AND HARDLY on purpose, I bled on Henry's sheets. By morning, the blood has already set, and like the blood of Duncan, it will not wash out. Yes, irreparable damage has been done, but it is only a sheet and a little bit on a pillowcase, which is barely noticeable. It isn't as if I've wrecked something that cannot be replaced, but still, Henry makes a fuss. "These are Egyptian cotton sheets," he wails. "Do you have any idea how much they cost?"

"It's not as if you can't still use them," I say. "So there's a stain. It's only menstrual blood."

Henry is not to be consoled. Like his sheets matter to him more than I do, and that he considers menstrual blood to be something disgusting. Like pus or vomit.

All of Max's sheets were stained. Stained, signed, and dated. The very first time I had occasion to say, "I've got my period," and Max dipped his finger inside me. With my blood, Max drew a heart on the sheet. The perimeters of love. Paleolithic art. Like the cave paintings at Lascaux. As primal as the beat of a drum, and by the time we were done for the night, there was blood everywhere. As if he'd made a meal of me and used the sheet for a napkin, and blood was on Max's hands and wrists and mouth and groin and thighs and chin and between his toes.

In the morning, Max stripped the sheet from the bed, but instead of putting it in the hamper along with his dirty clothes and towels, he spread it flat on the dining room table. As if it were a linen cloth and he were going to put out plates and silverware. Between the heart and a blot that could've been a piece of a Rorschach test, Max wrote with a felt-tip pen our names—Max and Lila—and the date.

O romance! O chivalry! O lift me off my feet and out of my head. Take my wrists and shackle me. Take my heart. My lungs. My liver. O love. Sweet and wondrous love. The stuff of bucolics, aubades, and canzones. Kisses like couplets, and pleasures of the idyll.

It wasn't until later, after we were married, that I had other thoughts about that. That I twisted a gesture of passion into thoughts concerning a German, a direct descendant of Albert Speer, making art of Jewish blood.

Nonetheless, Max did see beauty or truth or whatever in my blood whereas Henry sees only that I've soiled his sheets. The comparison is sorry, and before I can stop myself, and I do try to stop myself—a voice in my head admonishes me don't say that, *don't say that*—and then I say it. "You're turning into your Aunt Adele. You're like a pathetic old woman who has only her possessions. You're even starting to look like her, the way you're balding. You too will be wearing a wig soon enough."

Henry refuses to take the bait. Instead, he quietly apologizes for overreacting, and he sets out the breakfast dishes.

Over the sort of breakfast I never make for myself or for anyone else either—eggs, potatoes, English muffins with raspberry jam—Henry asks me, "Have you looked into getting yourself a new shrink yet?"

I swallow a bite of muffin and tell Henry, " I'm not getting another one."

Henry puts down his fork. "You don't think maybe you should? Maybe it would be good for you?"

"You don't just replace people like they are cars or refrigerators, Henry. One breaks and you go out and get yourself a new one. What? After Max died I should've immediately gone and gotten myself a new husband?"

"It's not the same thing," Henry says, but he's wrong about that. All loss leaves an empty space that cannot be filled, no matter who else comes along.

We finish our meal and, out of nowhere, Henry goes glum on me. He clams up, and I want to know, "What's with you? What's going on here?"

"I'm mad at you," he says, and I ask, "Why? For what reason? Because I don't want to replace Leon like he's a broken toaster or a worn-out bath mat?"

"No." Henry is curt. "From before." Henry is mad at me from before. "I'm mad at you from before breakfast. You said some pretty mean things, Lila. You can be cruel, you know."

Yes, I know this about myself. That I strike the first blow in the belief that it will save me from the onslaught. Only sometimes there is no onslaught, and I'm out there all alone just being nasty, is all. Whatever, that was before breakfast and here it is after breakfast, and I don't get why he is mad at me now. "If you were mad at me earlier," I ask, "why didn't you say something then?"

"Because," Henry explains, "I needed to get in touch with my emotions."

"You needed to get in touch with your emotions? And this quest, this search to find out what you were feeling, took you an hour and a half?"

"Yes," Henry says, and I say, "Tell me this, Henry. If we fuck now, does that mean you won't come until tomorrow?" As if an orgasm were a feeling like sad or happy instead of another kind of feeling. Whereas I might not distinguish the difference, I have a hunch that on the journey to find his feelings, Henry gets lost. He prefers to stay at home where he knows the terrain. Consequently, Henry does not know that flying off the handle can be an adventure, and he does not know what it is to succumb to the darkness. His feelings are like vegetation. Things that need water and direct sunlight and time to blossom. For Henry, anger is something with which he needs to get in touch. We are opposites that way. For me, anger is something from which I seek release. We are antonyms, Henry and I, which you'd think would make for a kind of compatibility, a balance, but it doesn't.

Henry excuses himself to take a shower. "I'm going to take a shower now," he says, and he gets up from the table. It is not Henry's fault that he can't love me in the only way I know how to be loved, the way I need to be loved, the kind of all-encompassing love that turned out to be way too much. It's not fair to fault Henry for not being Max.

While Henry showers, I go to change the sheets on his bed. It's the least I can do. He keeps his linens on the middle shelf of the hall closet, but my eye takes in all the shelves. There, on the top one, I spot the small, powder blue box tied with a white ribbon. Tiffany's. How sweet of him. He went to Tiffany's for my birthday gift, and I go all soft with gratitide.

I know it's wrong of me, but I can't help it. I have to peek. I untie the bow and lift the lid from the box. I blink in the hopes that I am seeing things because staring me in the face is a diamond. A diamond ring. An engagement ring. Eek! No! Oh, Henry! You fool. Why not earrings or a brooch? What are you trying to do? Ruin everything? What will I do? What will I say?

With haste and without attention to neatness, I retie the bow. I put the box back where I found it, and I flee from Henry's apartment.

31

rest: A term adapted from music and generally definable as a pause that counts in the metrical scheme. Most poets restrict this definition to situations where a pause compensates for the absence of an unstressed syllable or syllables in a foot. However, others have suggested that a rest may take the place of an entire foot.

"HI DAD," I SAY. "IT'S ME. LILA." I wait for the pause and then I add, "Your daughter."

"Oh. Lila. How are you?" my father asks.

"Good," I say. "And you?"

"Fine. It's ninety-one degrees outside, but in here it's seventy-two. We're climate controlled. So," he asks, "is there anything new with you?"

My father, even if pressed to remember, would not know the date of my birthday or that it is coming up. He would never know when to wish me a happy one or to send me a card. That was Bella's turf.

Already the cancer had set up primary residence in Bella's uterus, although no one yet knew it was there when I received what would be the last birthday card from my mother. The end card. It featured a childlike drawing of a girl. Not a stick figure, but a girl that could've been an illustration from a classic children's book.

Eloise or Madeline or Harriet. Only it wasn't any of them. It was just a drawing of some goofy, pink girl wearing a boater hat. A lone daisy clenched in her fist. On the inside flap of the card, in black block letters, was the message *Get Well Soon*, which my mother had X'd out with a blue pen. Beneath that, she wrote, "I didn't have my glasses on when I bought this. I thought it was a birthday card. Enjoy! Luv, Mom and Dad."

My mother had the eyesight of a hawk. She did not wear glasses. Not then. Not ever. Even as she was near to dying, and all else was failing her, her eyes remained sharp enough that she gestured me to bend so that she could whisper in my ear, "Lila. Your blouse. A stain." With effort, she pointed at where a splash of coffee had missed my mouth and landed on my collar.

Luv, Mom and Dad. Luv. Another Anglican affectation or an inability to go all the way with that word. Bella wrote *Luv, Mom and Dad.* She signed the card from the two of them, as if he had some part in it, but he didn't. Had I said to my father, "Thanks for the card," he would've said, "What card is that?"

Enclosed in the envelope along with the *Get Well Soon* card was a check for three hundred and fifty-seven dollars. An amount defying rational thought. An amount without rhyme or reason, but the gesture spoke volumes. Volumes in the shape of locusts and a pox upon my house. Along with the dicta regarding the atrocity of wearing white after Labor Day, of the obligation of pocketbooks to match shoes, and of never going to a dinner party emptyhanded was the one about cash gifts. "With the exceptions of weddings, bar mitzvahs, confirmations, graduations, the milestones, you never, ever give money as a present," my mother drill-instructed me in the Bella Morse book of manners. "Money," she said, "is a thoughtless gift. An insult, really."

Yes, I could have torn up the check into little pieces and maintained a semblance of dignity, but only the card went into the garbage. The check I took to the bank.

The following year on my birthday my mother was in the hospital, adrift in the lily pond that was morphine-derived, and really how can I expect my father to remember his daughter's birthday when he can barely remember that he's got a daughter. Still, I won't say that it doesn't sting just a little bit, that a bubble of blood doesn't rise to the surface where I am wounded, when before hanging up he says, "Okay then. Thank you for calling," and nothing else.

32

pastoral: an elaborately conventional poem expressing an urban poet's nostalgic image on the golden peace and simplicity of a pastoral existence.

I'D WARNED HIM, AND I TRIED my best to dissuade him from this weekend in the mountains. "No," I told Henry. "That's not a good plan. You should forget about it. Jews don't do well in the country. It's not for us. We're a ghetto people."

"Come on, Lila. You don't even go to temple or do anything Jewish. Besides, Jews do too vacation in the country. The Catskills are crawling with them."

"Whatever. *I* don't do well in the country. No rural landscapes for me. If I'm looking out over a body of water, I want to see garbage floating in it."

It was Henry's brainchild to take me for a prebirthday weekend getaway, which was all very nice as long as he was thinking getaway to Philadelphia, Boston, or Baltimore. As if the birds and bees carry disease rather than pollen through the fresh air, I avoid the countryside. Confronted with natural beauty, I become positively morose. When the sky is as dark as the abyss and soft as a lover's hand caressing the curve of the spine and the Milky Way weeps stars, so do I. Dawn peels away night along with my flesh. Birdsongs are melancholic melodies and crickets chirp alone. The loveliness haunts me.

The serenity gets inside and squeezes at my soul in a way that causes me to grieve. One winter I happened upon a waterfall frozen in flow. Such a sight, and it felt to me as if I were trapped in the white ice of the ninth circle. I'll pass on God's handiwork in favor of the mess man has made.

Not to mention I fear Henry has deliberately sought out an idyllic spot as the place to pop the question. He would do that, choose some sentimental setting. In the worst way, I don't want Henry to ask me to marry him. I'm not ready for that. Whatever answer I give him, it is sure to be the wrong one.

"Oh Lila. Come on, please," Henry said. "It's autumn already up there now. I don't have the kids this weekend. We can head out Thursday after your class. It'll be just you and me and the mountains and leaves crunching underfoot. Please."

Depending on the circumstances, I can be a pushover for a man who begs, and when Henry again said, "Please. We'll have a great time. I promise you," I said, "Okay. I'll go, but consider yourself warned."

Now Henry wants to take yet another walk in the woods, but I refuse to accompany him. One walk in the woods was plenty for me. Autumn's colors are death's palette, but Henry thinks it has to do with my shoes. "You didn't enjoy yourself before because you were wearing heels, Lila. No one walks in the woods wearing high heels. Change your shoes, and you'll see."

I'm not changing my shoes for a walk, nor do I agree to go for a bicycle ride along some godforsaken country lane that leads to nowhere. To look at a cow is reason enough to sob, and Henry, at a loss, throws up his hands. "Tell me then. What would you like to do?"

"Nothing. Go away." I say go away when what I want is for Henry to come to me, to hold me in his arms, to rub my back and kiss my face and neck. I want him to love me and care for me and stay with me, but I say, "Get lost. Leave me alone." I roll over and bury my face in the pillow, and Henry obliges me. He shuts the door behind him, but he is not gone for long. He is back with brochures he picked up at the front desk. "We can go to Cooperstown." He sits himself next to me. "It's not far from here. It's not a city, but the sidewalks are paved," he swears to it.

Home to the Baseball Hall of Fame, Cooperstown was built and designed for the tourist trade, and the concept is accommodated by the busload. A four-block stretch of a traffic jam, and the streets are lined with old-fashioned ice cream parlors, clip joints selling baseball memorabilia at top-dollar prices, and gift shops that reek of potpourri and scented candles. .

"Are you hungry?" Henry asks me, and I am. "Very hungry," I tell him.

At Long John Silver's, waiters dressed as pirates serve fried fish. I cannot dine comfortably at such a family-style theme eatery, but next door Doc Holiday's Wild West Burger Saloon treats its patrons to a mock shoot-out every hour on the hour. A strolling mariachi band hovers over you while you try to eat your taco at Pancho Villa's Cantina, and I tell Henry, "I prefer to starve."

We don't belong here. Henry and I don't fit in. We are not a part of the crowd. With Henry as the lone exception, the men and boys here wear baseball caps. The women favor jogging outfits in pastel colors. Pink, baby blue, pale yellow, and because these women are fat, they look like bales of cotton candy. Bales of cotton candy giving me the hairy eyeball. Like they never before in their lives saw a woman dressed in black kicking repeatedly at the base of the statue of Babe Ruth. I kick at the statue and I'm cursing Henry for bringing me here, to this place where everybody else is happy, where no one is alone, where they all are fans of baseball. The bales of cotton candy are not sure if I am something of a scandal or part of a Cooperstown exhibit, street theater, because supposedly Babe Ruth was an abusive husband. When Henry pulls me away, we get a smattering of tentative applause.

The drive home takes nearly four hours, and that is with Henry's foot hot on the gas pedal. We do not speak at all until we hit the Palisades Parkway and then I say, "I warned you. From the minute you dreamed up this scheme, I told you this would happen. I told you I don't do well in the country. You should have believed me."

"You really do need to get another therapist," Henry says. "You have so much love inside of you, Lila." Henry's voice is soft but detached. As if he were the professional offering his oh-so-professional opinion. As opposed to the guy whose dick I sucked five times in the last three days despite my foul mood. "You don't know what to do with the kind of love you have," he says. "You need an outlet for it, and I don't mean sex. Have you considered doing volunteer work?" he asks. "You know, with old people or maybe AIDS babies. Someone who needs the kind of love you have to give."

After taking a minute to think this over, I say, "Henry, go fuck yourself," and that is the full extent of our conversation until nothing but dumb luck lands Henry a parking spot on Washington Street. Halfway between his apartment and mine.

I get out of the car, and so does Henry. He pops open the trunk, and I lift my suitcase with both hands gripping the handle. It's very heavy because I overpacked. Like I was going somewhere nice for the weekend. That it is better to bring too much than not enough is yet another lesson I learned at my mother's knee, and Henry says, "Let me carry that for you."

"I prefer to carry it myself," I say, which is a lie, but a lie I have reason to tell.

"Come on. Let me carry it. I'll walk you home." As if he could ease my burden, Henry reaches for the suitcase, but I swing it to the left of his grasp the way a bullfighter taunts the bull with his cape, and I tell Henry, "I'm not going home."

The weight of the suitcase and my baggage—including four pairs of shoes, formal wear, a blow-dryer, and a travel iron—strain the muscles in my arms and shoulders. A slow burn, but I dare not rest it on the ground for fear that Henry will snatch it from me.

"You're not going home?" he asks. "It's after eleven on a Sunday night. Where are you going?"

"For a walk." I tell him that much.

"For a walk to where?"

I do not answer him, but I look off in the direction of the river.

"You're going to the river," Henry surmises. "Why? For what? It's dangerous there."

"That's the idea," I say.

Forget the implications here. Never would I throw myself into the Hudson River. It is not in my best interest to drown among the flotsam and jetsam and slicks of oil. Not to mention the used condoms, but I do want Henry to wonder. To be concerned enough to save me. To nudge him in that direction, I remind him that poets are famous for offing themselves. "I am of a tradition of suicides," I say. "It's practically expected of us."

"Lila," Henry says, "you do not want to die."

"Maybe not." I crank it up, the volume on the melodrama, and I add, "But I don't feel much like living either."

Henry makes another grab for my suitcase, but he winds up holding on to a handful of air. "Stop this," he insists. "Come on now. Go home. Get some sleep. You'll feel better tomorrow."

I say I won't feel better tomorrow and Henry says that I will feel better tomorrow and we volley this back and forth as if tomorrow were a Ping-Pong ball until I say, "Henry, leave me alone."

Henry turns and heads off in the direction of his apartment. I hoist my suitcase and take three steps toward the river before I stop. I'm giving Henry time to catch up with me. To be back at my side. Like a guardian angel or a leech, which I will welcome because I am ready now to quit this nonsense and let Henry carry my suitcase home for me. I am ready to sleep. I want to sleep in Henry's bed, the two of us nestled together like a pair of spoons.

I look in all directions but I don't see Henry anywhere, and I panic that he's gone to do something sensible, such as call the police or Bellevue Hospital to come and get me. The sort of thing you are supposed to do when you've got a suicide threat on your hands and on your conscience.

My suitcase bangs against my shins as I hurry as fast as I can to get to Henry before he makes a big deal of this. I backtrack to where his car is parked and then race to his apartment. I'm going to have bruises on my legs from my ankles up to my thighs and down again.

From the street three flights below, I see that Henry's kitchen light is on. I push open the heavy glass door to the lobby and I press 3F. "It's me, Henry," I speak into the intercom.

Rather than waiting for the elevator to make its way down from the top floor, I take the stairs. Hauling my suitcase up the three flights leaves me short of breath. Henry is waiting for me by the open door, and between gasps of air I say, "I thought you were calling the police. Or Bellevue."

"No. I wasn't calling anyone." Henry blocks the threshold to his apartment as if he's barring me entry. As if he wants to keep this and me out of his home and in the hall. His shirt is off. His shoes are off too, and he's eating Doritos from the bag. The crunch of the chips is loud. "I had to take a leak something fierce," he says. "And I wanted to check my messages. I was going to come look for you after I had something to eat. I was starving."

In the time it took for him to urinate, to check his messages, and to stuff his face with chips, I could've killed myself three times over. Had I made good on my implied threat, he'd have come looking for me only to find me floating facedown in the river, bobbing like a buoy by the Christopher Street pier. There are no words available with which to respond to him. I open my mouth, but in a stranglehold of impediment, my tongue is as numb as the rest of me. I am utterly speechless, and Henry shifts uneasily as if he fears I might now do something rash and violent, such as kill him, and he says to me, "I don't know what's eating at you, Lila. But whatever it is, you have to somehow try and forgive yourself."

Reaching out, I snatch the bag of Doritos away from him as if depriving him of sustenance were all that remained for me to do. "And you can forget about me marrying you. I'd never marry you," I say, and Henry closes the door.

33

....

hysteron proteron: (Greek "later earlier"). A figure in which
the natural order of time in which events occur is reversed, usually because the latter event is considered more important than
the former: in Shakespeare's phrase, "for I was bred and born";
also found in Virgil, "Let us die and rush into battle."

THE STEAM FROM FRESH TAR
wafts with the breeze and it smells like burning rubber or like a
neighborhood in perdition. The end of summer, and it is official
now. Not because the school year has begun nor has it anything to
do with the solstice. It's the paving over of Hudson Street that
marks the summer's finale. As if hell were closing up shop for the
cold seasons, a *Gone Fishing* sign posted over the pit.

Above the din of the traffic I relay to Carmen the story of my
weekend away with Henry, but Carmen is not impressed. "What did
you expect from him? Passion? Hysteria? An emotional outburst on
the street? In public? No, no, never. Henry," she notes, "is of Anglo-
Episcopal stock."

We descend the stairs into the subway station. Our train pulls
in, and we grab ourselves a pair of seats. Without missing a beat,
Carmen picks up where she left off. "You can bank on it," she says.
"You go to throw yourself into the river to drown, and the Anglo-
Episcopal will go home to have a pee and a snack. The way they see

it, you were quite determined. Which leaves them with nothing to do but keep a stiff upper lip and get on with their lives. Cheerio, ta-ta, and all that. So," she asks, "what are you going to do? Are you going to forgive him? He can't help himself, you know. He was born into it."

Carmen has made a composite study of ethnic stereotypes, and she swears by these prejudices of hers. What prevents her from out-right bigotry is that she passes no judgment. Of her own people, the Paraguayans, she says, "We're a lot like the Argentines. We lean to-ward a Spanish tradition, especially that of the Inquisition. We can't help it. We're crazy for a fascist. A uniform makes our blood bub-ble." Such was Carmen's rationale for her assessment of Max. "Yes, he is arrogant," she said, "and yes he enjoyed having you locked in the closet, but that is the way a German knows to love." Then she apologized to me. "I can't help myself there either. Give a Paraguayan a Nazi and we'll offer him refuge every time."

Of the English, Carmen contends they are like rain, and at the core, Henry is of his heritage.

There is nothing for which to forgive Henry. I treated him badly. I wanted him to love me, but I wouldn't let him love me. "I don't know," I say to Carmen. "The fit wasn't right, is all. It had to end at some point. It was never like it was with Max," and she says, "This is our stop."

Carmen and I exit the subway at Times Square, and I look around long enough to be disgusted. "Do you believe what they've done to this place? What a hellhole." What they—the mayor, the real estate developers, and the Disney Corporation—have done is to sanitize Times Square. They rid the area of whores, pimps, junkies, religious fanatics, schizophrenics, and weirdos as if these people were termites. The grand old porno palaces, the movie theaters that packed the house with perverts for matinee showings of *Teenage Lesbian Pep Squad* and *Bubble Butt Bonanza: The Sequel* have been scrubbed free of jizz stains and now feature family fare. Times Square, once synonymous with sleaze, is on its way to being the

Zurich of New York City. Clean as soap and the place to go for a cup of hot cocoa. "It's a scandal"—I shake my head in disgust—"what they've done to this neighborhood."

"Why do you care?" Carmen wants to know. "It's not like Times Square was your home away from home. When was the last time you were here for any reason?"

Before Max and I got married, before the time that I restricted my range, Max and I took a walk along Eighth Avenue and across 42nd Street. Passing an XXX-rated video store, we paused at the sign which covered the window like a shade. *We have Lesbian, Group, Men, Amateur, Bondage, Bestiality, Discipline, Anal, Straight, and German*, it read.

"What is that?" I asked Max. "German as a kind of sex. What does that mean? Have you been holding out on me?"

"I have no idea what that is about," Max said. "Really," he insisted when I was slow to believe his ignorance. "I never heard of such a thing."

Always eager to broaden my horizons, I dragged Max inside to make a purchase. Which made Max jittery as if he were going to be arrested and humiliated in public. As if his face were going to show up on the evening news. Which I thought was so adorable of him.

Clutching our German videotape in the requisite brown paper bag, we hurried back to Max's apartment to learn what there was to Max's culture that we'd been missing out on.

Max popped the tape into the VCR, and he came and sat next to me on the couch to watch what was either a home movie or very poor production quality. Not to mention that there wasn't much in the way of star quality either. Two unattractive men—one lean with hair on his back and the other beer-bellied—and two women notable only for being heavy-breasted were sucking, fucking, switching partners, and fucking and sucking some more. Tame stuff, and it would have been tedious too had they not been speaking in German. It was the German language which lent the film that special something. A kink. A context which was lost on Max. "I do not understand this," he said. "Why should this be a separate category?"

"Because," I explained, "they're speaking German. There are associations to that. And connotations. Like the idea of Germans having sex is depraved in and of itself. Like it has to be sick because it is German."

Although most decent people are loath to admit it, we do have an ongoing fascination, an enthusiasm, regarding things German. Something like the way children can't help but examine what they've extricated from their noses or the way the general public can't get enough gory detail of a gruesome crime. The way we devoured the story of Jeffrey Dahmer's cannibalism with no less of an appetite than Jeffrey had for his victims. Face the facts. Nazis are big business. Forged diaries and biographies sell like hotcakes, and at country fairs all across America you find families lining up to pay a dollar per head to touch the leather interior of Hitler's Mercedes.

Still, Max remained baffled, and we did not watch the film in its entirety because it bored him. Plus, we didn't need it.

I tell Carmen that not being a Times Square denizen does not deny me a moral imperative. "I've never gone camping in the Grand Canyon," I say, "but that doesn't mean I'm all for converting it into a multilevel parking garage. It's embarrassing here. We've got to be the only major international city without a red-light district."

For reasons beyond me, synthetic dog poop, plastic vomit, and T-shirts proclaiming sexual dysfunction are not offensive to the sensibilities. The novelty shops have been spared the wrecking ball and are open for business as usual. Carmen holds the door for me, and she directs me to the back of the store.

There are the paraphernalia and machinery needed for the production and purchase of counterfeit credentials. Xeroxed university diplomas, bogus certificates of achievement, and ersatz identification cards. The line is long with teenagers seeking entry into the state of inebriation. Ah, to drink from the holy grail or, better yet, straight from the bottle. These teens are after identification cards which will prove them to be twenty-one years of age, the magic number which will enable them to buy hooch to drink themselves stupid, and I tell Carmen, "I must be the only one here who wants to be younger."

In a glass case, stacked in neat piles and ready to be filled in with the pertinent data and passport-size photos, are copies, indistinguishable from the originals, of student I.D. cards from New York University, St. John's University, and Manhattanville College.

"Take your pick." The man working the counter is Korean with a Brooklyn accent.

"My friend needs a driver's license," Carmen says, but he shakes his head emphatically. "No way, babe. No can do. A driver's license. That's against the law."

Carmen leans in, her elbows resting on the glass case. "Let me get this straight," she says. "A phony driver's license is against the law, but supplying teenagers with dummy I.D. so they can do some serious underage drinking is within legal bounds. Have I got that right?"

His gaze darts over our heads and around the shop. It's as if he's thinking he might be the target of a sting investigation and that Carmen and I are a pair of undercover cops or journalists out to expose illicit business. He's on the lookout for the hidden cameras, and ball bearings of perspiration appear on his forehead and upper lip.

"Relax," I tell him. "We're not the law, but this is the deal here. I'm about to turn thirty-five. I want a legitimate-looking piece of paper that puts me at thirty-two. What can you do for me?"

"Thirty-five?" he says. "No way you're thirty-five. You got to be bullshitting me. You look like one of these kids." He cocks his thumb at the line snaking behind me.

I run my fingers through my hair and flash a smile, which is an involuntary reflex action. The response to flattery for which I am a sucker. "Can't you help me out? Please," I coo at him. My lower lip is wet and it pouts, and apparently he is something of a sucker too. He disappears behind a curtain and returns with a New York County identification card.

Never before having seen such a thing, I ask him, "What is this? Since when does New York County require its citizens to carry papers?" I wonder if mine will be stamped *Jüdin*.

"It's legitimate," he assures me. "It's for people who have no other form of I.D. You know, you don't drive so you don't have a driver's license. You never been off the block, so who's got a passport? But you got to have something with your picture on it, so you get issued one of these at the courthouse."

"Which courthouse?" I ask. "At Supreme Court?"

"How do I know which courthouse? What do I look like? A judge?" he says. "All I know is that it's good."

Carmen and I exchange a glance and she says, "It looks legit to me."

I spell out my name, my social security number, and my altered date of birth for the Korean man from Brooklyn who types the information in on the appropriate lines. After he snaps my photograph, he laminates the whole shebang and hands me the card for my approval.

"Yeah." I am impressed. "This should do the trick." Like how in therapy you need to go back before you can go ahead or the way a watch is wound.

"For you," he says, "thirty bucks. No tax." He holds his hand out, palm up, and Carmen pays him with three tens. After snatching the identification from my grasp, Carmen asks the man for a bag, which she folds around the card as if gift-wrapping it before giving it back to me. "I know that good advice is wasted on the young," Carmen says to me, "but try to spend your youth wisely. And," she instructs, "you're not to use this until your birthday."

Having elevated what is either petty vanity or some manifestation of neurosis into a riddle for a Zen master, I contemplate the conundrum before me: that I must wait two days to be three years younger than I am now.

34

topos: A commonplace appropriate for literary treatment, an intellectual theme suitable for development and modification according to the imagination of the individual author.

AT THE PODIUM, I SHUFFLE papers as if I am busy with that. What I am really up to is a head count. Never have I recovered fully from my early days on the reading circuit. As indelibly etched as a tattoo on my ego is the mortification of having no one—not one person—come out to hear me read at the Great Jones Book House. How I stood there looking out at row upon row upon row of empty seats off into infinity. Which may, or may not, have been more awful than those times I had an audience of two or three people, if you count Carmen and the homeless man who came in not for poetry but for warmth.

To be up there looking out on empty seats causes your face to scorch from shame, but soon I am able to relax. The room fills with bodies, and a gaggle of college girls resort to sitting cross-legged on the floor.

I open with a poem called "The Seven Steps to Self-Gratification," a Sicilian septet which rhymes *ababab*, and then I read a couple of sonnets and a sestina which was inspired by Max's mouth and features. Wet, heat, salt, ravish, harsh, and tongue as the six end words.

If you think of T. S. Eliot, most often "The Wasteland" comes to mind. Alan Ginsburg gets you "Howl," and William Carlos Williams is forever hitched to his red wheelbarrow in the rain, and were I to dare include myself in such a cluster of luminaries, I am best known for an epyllion. A little epic, in dactylic hexameter, titled "At the Baby Doll Lounge Salome Dances; The Baptist Tips Her a Ten Spot." It's my crowd pleaser, that with which they are familiar, the way you perk up to a song when you know the lyrics, which is why I save it for last. So they'll leave happy and humming the tune.

With a practiced modesty, I say thank you and I absorb the applause, which is followed by a question-and-answer period.

One of the college girls on the floor wants to know if I write on a computer. Someone always asks that question, and I would love to ask what the hell kind of difference it makes, but instead I am gracious. "I write longhand," I say, in present tense as if it were something I'm doing still. "Pen to paper. I write on yellow legal pads. Write and rewrite, drawing arrows and brackets, and huge red X's with each draft. Only when I am satisfied that a poem is finished do I enter it into the computer and run it through spell-check before printing it out. I can't spell worth a damn." A small confession which elicits titters from the audience.

It's an assumption, and a wrong one to boot, that those of us who live by the written word are good spellers, that our grammar is unfailingly proper, that our punctuation is precise, that our participles never dangle.

"But you're a writer," the girl says. Like there is a connection between how words are spelled and the music they make.

"Poor spelling," I explain, "is an offshoot of creative vision. I see the multiplicity of possibilities in the convention." Sometimes I slay myself, what with the kind of crap I can spew.

A woman with braided hair and reading glasses perched at the end of her nose raises her hand. "Do you write every day?" she asks.

"Yes." I tell a whopping big lie. So big that it tweaks at my nose, and quickly I move on to the young man who asks, "How much money do poets make?" To him, I tell the truth. "None," I say. "Or at least not enough that it's worth mentioning."

"Did you really dance topless at the Baby Doll Lounge?" Another one of the college girls is contemplating a career move, no doubt.

I smile as if I've got a secret, and I say, "I refuse to answer on the grounds that it could incriminate me."

That I never danced topless at the Baby Doll Lounge or anyplace else either is not what they want to hear. Although the poem is written in first-person narrative, it was a college chum of mine, Tara, who shook her booty for drunken fraternity boys and conventioneers from Columbus, Ohio. In a kind of Faustian deal, I appropriated a slice of Tara's lifetime and made it my own. With the bargain, I achieved infamy and she got respectability.

Now even Tara believes I was the topless dancer because she is married to a bond salesman. They live in a Brooklyn Heights brownstone with their two children and a giant schnauzer named Snuffles. The two children are boys with carrot red hair and upturned noses which are conduits for overwhelming amounts of mucus. Tara's pockets bulge with crumpled tissues. She is co-president of the PTA, and she can no longer imagine that half-naked and up on a runaway she danced to a disco beat. However, it's a snap for her to imagine that half-naked and up on a runaway *I* danced to a disco beat and then went home to write a poem about the experience of it.

Lovely as it's been, I've had my fill of this. I announce there is time for one more question, which is also my way of signaling to Carmen that we'll be out of here pronto. She is taking me for an eve-of-birthday dinner. Four hands go up, and I give the go-ahead to an older gentleman in the middle row because he is wearing a gray suit and striped tie. I like that. "I was curious," he asks, "as to what compels you to write exclusively in form?"

To answer him, I start at the beginning. With Aristotle, and how iambs are heartbeats and pulsebeats. Intrinsic rhythms, and as fundamental to our being as the breath we draw. To write in form is natural. And natural selection follows. Darwinian, if you consider the variations away from the iamb providing a platform upon which a natural selection can work. Not to mention how nature enjoys weeding out the weak. The form is cruel and does not forgive. The exactness has a purpose and ensures survival. Then I quote Jean Cocteau, "True freedom must be won within the confines of the rules."

There is freedom within the confines of form the way a barrier protects you from the elements of disaster. The way there is love in the bonds of marriage. "Without boundaries, you can be only adrift," I say. "Lost. Without lines drawn on the map, you are nowhere. It is better to be a prisoner of war than to be without a nation, a place, a people. If you will indulge me an analogy here," I say. "Think of a domestic bird. A canary. A pretty yellow canary. When you open the door to the birdcage, some canaries take off. Head straight for the open window and never look back. Ah, yes. The canary is free. The way birds ought to be, you say. The canary can fly anywhere it chooses to go. Far, far away. The sky is the limit, but you have to wonder if they later regret this choice they've made because it is cold out there. Not to mention predators, and there isn't any available birdseed, and where is that plastic ball with the bell of which they were so fond? They're lost, they panic, they flounder, and often have a head-on collision with a pane of glass. In the cage, safe and warm and well fed, they are free to sing and to warble. To make music. Maybe they should stay in their cages and sing their hearts out. Unbridled passion," I bang my fist on the podium, and take myself completely by surprise. "Unbridled passion results from being tied to the bedpost. Release serves only to deliver you from love. Unhanded and you are alone in the world," and then I say, "Max," and my hand goes to my mouth as if I've burped. "Thank you all very much," I say, "but you'll have to excuse me now. I have a plane to catch."

Carmen stops me at the exit, taking hold of my sleeve. "A plane to catch?" she asks.

"Yes. A plane to catch."

Carmen smiles and she says, "Have a happy birthday, Lila." Like I've said, Carmen and I encourage one another. I smile with gratitude, and then I am gone. Gone.

35

---

epicedium: A song of mourning in praise of the dead, sung in the presence of the corpse and distinguished from *threnos*, a dirge, which was not limited by time or place.

Because wonderful things happen serendipitously without apparent forethought or plan, I will not consider here what it is I am doing or any possibilities as to where it will lead us. All I'll say is that with my American Express card, my fake I.D., and in seat 27A on the 11:53 plane out to Los Angeles, I am going back in years. It's always been symmetrical, the mathematical equation for the movement of time. It goes forward, and now it's going backward too. I'm going to go back to Max. I'm going to fall into his arms and tell him I love him, that I never stopped loving him, and that we'll be together always. Then, I hope, I can persuade him to leave Los Angeles. We belong in New York.

I stare out the window into the black sky. There is nothing to see out there other than the vastness of the night and the glimmer of my reflection coming back at me, like a refrain, from the glass. I turn away from what my double might have to say and my stomach lurches, jumping like a bean. Anticipation, or perhaps only the result of the plane beginning its descent.

At Los Angeles International Airport, I have no luggage to collect. Instead, I find the ladies' room and try to collect myself. Standing over a sink, I splash cold water on my face and wipe away smudges of mascara. A fresh coat of lipstick does little to relieve the overall finish of gray. As a result of the recycled air in the plane, my skin is ashen and without luster, and beneath my eyes, like a pair of *breves,* two unstressed syllables, dark crescent moons mark the fatigue. I'm a weary and haggard traveler, but no matter. Max is accustomed to me this way. Like death passing over.

Crossing the terminal to a battery of stainless-steel phone stalls, I open the local directory to the S's. As if it were written in Chinese, I run my finger from the top of the page to the bottom, scanning the columns. S-a, S-c, S-c-h, and I find Max Schirmer listed at 407 Sunnyview Terrace, which is kind of amusing given how Max's temperament is anything but sunny-viewed. I copy the address on the back of an envelope.

Past the Hertz Rent A Car station and Avis too, I exit through the glass door beneath the taxi sign. I don't know my way around Los Angeles, and this is no time to get lost. Not to mention it is no time to get myself killed, which could happen were I to drive the freeways here.

"Luggage?" The driver is standing by the trunk of his cab, and I tell him I haven't any luggage. I tell him where I wish to go. I lean into the backseat, and we're off. Like a thoroughbred horse nearing the finish line, my pulse races and I could snort from the desire. The end, the happy end, is near. So near.

The cab pulls up to the curb, and I check the address, number 407 illuminated beneath a porch light, against that on the envelope because there has to be some mistake. Could it be that there are two Max Schirmers in the Los Angeles area? A trim split-level house painted white is no place for my Max to be living. Manicured hedges flank the yard, and there are bursts of flowerbeds which are free of weeds. A lone palm tree punctuates the start of the driveway like an exclamation point at the wrong end of a sentence. I follow the path to the door, and I imagine someday Max and I laughing about how he once lived in such a house.

The doorbell chimes a melody, and the first hint of the morning peeks out over the horizon. As if the horizon were a wall to climb, and the smog for which Los Angeles is famous renders the event a ribbon of pink and purple. Exquisite colors fashioned from the decay and the doom.

It is apparent that I have roused Max from his bed. My Max. Not some other Max. Wearing gym shorts, and his eyelids are heavy with sleep. "Hi," I say. "Remember me?"

Maybe he's having a bout of gas. Like maybe those lentils are finally catching up to him, because he isn't looking any too pleased here.

"It's me, Lila," I say. "Your wife," to which he says, "Ex-wife."

This isn't exactly how I pictured our reunion. The way I pictured it, by this point we'd be hugging and kissing and bluebirds would be singing and we'd be well on our way to boinking in the bushes already. "Max," I take a deep breath, "I'm sorry."

From inside his house, a voice calls out, "Max? Max? What's going on? Are you okay? Max?" It's a woman's voice, and she comes to the door too. She stands next to Max, and she is tall. Nearly as tall as he is. Her blond hair is tangled, but still I can tell it is silky hair when combed. I look for the dark roots, but there are none. She must have had a touch-up only yesterday. She is wearing a bathrobe, but instead of cinching it at the waist, the sash is tied beneath her breasts, defining the watermelon shape of her belly. She is pregnant. Very pregnant. I was not prepared for this. For her. For them. I did not know, and would never have guessed.

"This is Lila Moscowitz," Max tells her, and to me he says, "Lila. This is Dawn." For an instant, I am confused. Like I'm mixing her up with Henry's ex-wife. Only Max's Dawn has a chin and is very attractive if you go in for the type. "Dawn is my wife," Max adds. Like I hadn't figured that one out already.

I am at a loss to explain myself. I avert my gaze from the pair of them, fixing my eyes on a crack on the step and I say, "Well, I was in the neighborhood so I thought I'd pop by and say hello. That's all. So hello." Not to mention I am devastated.

"Where is your car?" Max quizzes me. "Or did you walk here?"

"I took a taxi," I say, and Max pounces on the inconsistency. "So you were not exactly in the neighborhood, were you?"

Dawn rests her hand on Max's arm, and she explains, "Max is very precise about geographical boundaries. To him, the neighborhood has definite parameters. It's the result of his profession. He's a cartographer," she tells me.

"Yes," I say. "I know that," and I must be shooting looks of poison darts aimed at the spot between her eyes because she backs away and sidesteps. Half-hidden behind Max, she says, "You will have to excuse me, but I've got to get ready for work. I'm a schoolteacher," she tells me. "Second grade." As if I'd asked. As if I cared. "It was really nice meeting you, Lila. Have a great day!"

Before Dawn is entirely out of earshot, I ask Max, "So? So when did this happen? When did you get married again?"

"It will be ten months next week," he tells me, and I say, "How nice for you."

"Yes," Max concurs. "It is very nice."

"So there's no use sweeping up after spilled milk. Is that it?"

"There's no use *crying* over spilled milk," Max tells me. "That is how the saying goes." Max folds his arms across his chest. His bare chest, and I swallow hard. Since when did Max, my Max, learn his proverbial expressions?

His bare chest where I had rested my head for so many nights, and after a few eternal seconds, I say, "This is kind of ridiculous, isn't it? Me standing here on your doorstep. Like we are two people who barely know one another instead of . . ."

"Yes," Max does not let me finish the thought. "It is very ridiculous."

A flash of anger flares in me, and I welcome the release it brings. "You can't pretend that I'm nobody to you. As if I'm a stranger who showed up on your doorstep one morning. We went through things together, and I have the scars to prove it." I start to roll up my sleeve as if there were needle tracks to show to him. "You can't forget, Max. Just because you've moved on into this house with flowerbeds and a sweet wife doesn't mean you can whitewash the past. You can't forget about us, Max. You can't just deny us. You can't just go on like nothing ever happened."

"Oh, but I can," Max says, and I say, "Oh, yeah. Right. I forgot. You people are good at that," which was not what I meant to say, and I try to take it back. "I didn't mean that," I say. "Forget I said that, okay?"

Max looks as if he's about to speak, but he doesn't have to. As if I were wearing X-ray glasses, I see the small stone lodged in the muscle of his heart. A small stone with my name on it. He glances at his wrist but he is not wearing a watch.

At the very least, I want to ask for his forgiveness. To forgive me for walking out on him and out on our love, but I am afraid to say that. Afraid of what will come next. Instead I smile and I say, "I guess you're not inviting me in for a cup of coffee or anything?" to which Max says, "It's not the same here as it is in New York." I assume he is referring to the fact that he no longer loves me at all, but then he adds, "Do you want me to call a car service for you? In Los Angeles you cannot hail a cab on the street."

"Yes," I say. "Thank you," and Max closes the door, and I call after him, "Aren't you going to wish me a happy birthday?"

I walk the length of the driveway, where I sit on the curb beside the palm tree, which looks like a fake the way it rises ridiculously from a spot where there ought to be an elm tree or a maple. There I sit to wait for the car to come and get me, to take me away from this. I sit with my knees pulled to my chest, and I bury my face there and I weep. I rock to and fro on the step of the curb as if I could console myself, and I say, "Shhh. Shhh." My face is wet with my tears when a lime-green hatchback pulls up and its horn toots like a toy. Like it's a giant M&M designed to shuttle passengers around Candyland or a miniature golf course or from cloud to cloud. Because I'm not sure if this car is for real, I check the windshield for a hack license, which is taped to the glass.

I sniffle and I wipe at my nose and at my eyes and I get into the silly car. The backseat doesn't afford much leg room. I shift and twist trying to find a way to get comfortable. The driver turns to me. He is young, and his long hair is tied back in a ponytail with a rawhide cord. He is wearing a Hawaiian shirt with pineapples on it, and he wants to know, "Where to?"

"Good question," I say, and then I ask, "Tell me. If it were your birthday today, where would you go?"

"Disneyland." He doesn't hesitate.

36

---

envoi: A short concluding stanza repeating the metrical half-stanza which precedes it, as well as the rhyme scheme of that half-stanza. It also repeats the refrain which runs through the poem.

FIRST, THE IRONY: I LOST THREE hours by traveling back east. Not to mention the traffic on the Long Island Expressway, and my birthday is half over before I even get my key in the door.

Still, there is time enough left to the day, and I get going with the preparations. From the freezer, I take out a Sara Lee coffee cake which has been in there forever and then some. It's frozen like the Ice Age, and the walnuts have set like rocks. I get a bottle of wine, and next, I get the plates. My good plates. Mismatched, not of a set, but they are all cobalt blue. I put nine cobalt blue cake plates out around the table, and I think about Passover. Yet another holiday my family did not celebrate, but still somewhere along the line I picked up bits and pieces of what's done. Like how a cup of wine is set on the table for the prophet Elijah. Plus, the door is left ajar for him, although you'd think a prophet would know to knock. Whatever. Elijah has yet to make an appearance at anyone's seder. Year in and year out, he's expected only he never shows, yet they don't give up on him.

That sort of faith, where you hang in there regardless, I never knew it. I never believed, but it can happen that faith comes organically from ritual. If an atheist prays daily, eventually God will hear the prayers.

Fetching Meryl from the closet, I hold the toy monkey to my breast. As if our hearts beat together, I carry Meryl to the dining area. Meryl is dwarfed in the chair, but Meryl is going to be dwarfed in size wherever. The remaining place settings are for Dora, Estella, Henry, Leon, Max, my father, me, and Bella, who may or may not show up. My mother was funny about last-minute invitations. As if spontaneity were an insult.

I strike a match to light the candles, which are neither birthday candles for making wishes nor Yahrzeit candles for mourning, but two white tapers. Which happen to be the only candles I've got and therefore they suit the occasion, which is a mixed bag of birth and burial and laying the dead, the near-dead, the once-dead, and the dying to rest. I need to tell them, all of them, that, each in my own way, I loved them dearly, but they've got to go now. They, and I, must rest in peace. Not to mention how forward movement is hindered when you've got the past hanging on, holding it back like that.

Also, I ought to admit here that the story about Dora and Estella spitting blood into hankies which Dora had embroidered with thread of purple silk, I made it up. For all I know, they spit up blood into old rags. The same as for all I know they lived not in my apartment but in the building across the street or down the block. I made up the part about how I live in what was once their apartment. They did live on Morton Street but no one remembered in which building, let alone if it were 5C in this building. It is true only that for too long I have lived with ghosts, and contrary to popular opinion, ghosts, like thoughts and dreams and words, do indeed have form.

Made in the USA
Lexington, KY
21 December 2012